PENGUIN MODERN CLASSICS

1518

THE OUTSIDER

Albert Camus was born in Algeria in 1913 of Breton and Spanish parentage. He was brought up in North Africa and had many jobs there (one of them playing in goal for the Algiers football team) before he came to Metropolitan France and took up journalism. He was active in the resistance during the German occupation and became editor of the clandestine paper *Combat*. Before the war he had written a play *Caligula* (1939), and during the war the two books which brought him fame, *L'Etranger* (*The Outsider*, 1942) and *Le Mythe de Sisyphe* (1942). Abandoning politics and journalism he devoted himself to writing and established an international reputation with such books as *La Peste* (*The Plague*, 1947), *Les Justes* (1949), *L'Homme révolté* (1952), and *La Chute* (*The Fall*, 1956). He was awarded the Nobel Prize for Literature in 1957. In January 1960 he was killed in a road accident.

ALBERT CAMUS

THE OUTSIDER

Translated by
STUART GILBERT

With an Introduction by
CYRIL CONNOLLY

PENGUIN BOOKS
in association with Hamish Hamilton

Penguin Books Ltd, Harmondsworth, Middlesex, England
Penguin Books Australia Ltd, Ringwood, Victoria, Australia

—

L'Etranger first published 1942
This translation first published in Great Britain by
Hamish Hamilton 1946
Published in Penguin Books 1961
Reprinted 1962, 1963 (twice), 1964, 1965, 1966, 1968

—

Copyright © the Estate of Albert Camus, 1942

—

Made and printed in Great Britain
by Hunt Barnard & Co. Ltd, Aylesbury
Set in Monotype Bembo

INTRODUCTION
To the First English Edition (1946)

The Outsider is the first book of a writer, now in his middle thirties, who played a notable part in the French Resistance Movement, who edited the daily paper, *Combat*, and whose name has been closely linked with Jean-Paul Sartre in the forefront of the new philosophical and realistic school of French literature. As well as this novel, Albert Camus has produced between 1942 and 1944 two plays, *Caligula* and *Le Malentendu*,[1] and a book of essays, *Le Mythe de Sisyphe*.[2] But he has an even more distinctive quality which colours all his work. He is an Algerian.

What is an Algerian? He is not a French colonial, but a citizen of France domiciled in North Africa, a man of the Mediterranean, an *homme du midi* yet one who hardly partakes of the traditional Mediterranean culture, unlike Valéry whose roots spread from Sète by way of Montpellier to Genoa; for him there is no eighteenth century, no baroque, no renaissance, no crusades or troubadours in the past of the Barbary Coast; nothing but the Roman Empire, decaying dynasties of Turk and Moor, the French Conquest and the imposition of the laws and commerce of the Third Republic on the ruins of Islam. It is from a sultry and African corner of Latin civilization that *The Outsider* emerges, the flower of a pagan and barrenly philistine culture. This *milieu* has a certain affinity with the Key West of Hemingway, or Deep South of Faulkner and Caldwell, with those torrid American cities where 'poor whites' exist uneasily beside poor blacks. In fact the neo-paganism which

1. *Two Plays*, London (Hamish Hamilton), 1946.
2. *The Myth of Sisyphus*, London (Hamish Hamilton), 1955.

is common to both civilizations, together with Camus' rapid and somewhat colloquial style, have caused some critics to consider *The Outsider* merely as a French exercise in the American 'tough guy' manner. But the atmosphere is not really similar. *The Outsider* is not at all a morbid book, it is a violent affirmation of health and sanity, there are no monsters, no rapes, no incest, no lynchings in it; it is the reflection, on the whole, of a happier society. Monsieur Sartre, asked in a recent interview if his friend Camus is also an 'existentialist', replied, 'No. That's a grave misconception. Although he owes something to Kierkegaard, Jaspers, and Heidegger, his true masters are the French moralists of the seventeenth century. He is a classical Mediterranean. I would call his pessimism "solar" if you remember how much black there is in the sun. The philosophy of Camus is a philosophy of the absurd, and for him the absurd springs from the relation of man to the world, of his legitimate aspirations to the vanity and futility of human wishes. The conclusions which he draws from it are those of classical pessimism.'

We possess a valuable piece of evidence which bears out this theory. In 1936 and 1937 Camus wrote two or three essays which have since been reprinted as *Les Noces*. No writer can avoid in his first essays the mention of the themes which are crystallizing for his later work. Two melodies emerge in these papers, a passionate love for Algiers and for the harsh meridional ecstasy which youth enjoys there, and also an anger and defiance of death and of our northern emphasis upon it. These are the two keys to *The Outsider*.

Le bourreau étrangla le Cardinal Carrafa avec un cordon de soie qui se rompit – il fallut y revenir deux fois. Le Cardinal regarda le bourreau sans daigner prononcer un mot.

STENDHAL, *La Duchesse de Palliano*

This quotation at the head of *Les Noces* might stand as a motto for the novel.

In his essay *Summer in Algiers*[1] Camus introduces us to the kind of *milieu* we will meet in the later book.

Men find here throughout all their youth a way of living commensurate with their beauty. After that, decay and oblivion. They've staked all on the body and they know that they must lose. In Algiers, for those who are young and alive, everything is their haven and an occasion for excelling – the bay, the sun, the red and white checkerboard of terraces going down to the sea, the flowers and stadiums, the fresh brown bodies. . . . But for those whose youth is past no place exists, no sanctuary to absorb their melancholy.

Farther on he gives a brief account of the ethics of these athletes.

The notion of hell, for instance, is here no more than a silly joke. Such imaginings are only for the very virtuous. And I am convinced that the word virtue is entirely meaningless throughout Algeria. Not that its men are without principles. They have their moral code. We don't 'chuck' our mothers, we make our wife respected in the street, we are considerate to the pregnant, we don't attack an enemy two against one, because it's 'cheap'. Whoever doesn't keep these elementary commandments 'is not a man' and the business is settled.

There are words whose meaning I have never clearly understood [he continues], such as the word sin. I know enough, however, to see that these men have never sinned against life, for if there is a sin against life, it is not perhaps so much to despair of life, as to hope for another life and to lose sight of the implacable grandeur of this one. These men have not cheated; lords of the Summer at twenty through their joy of living, though deprived of all hope they are gods still. I have seen two die, horrified but silent. It is better so. That is the rude lesson of the Algerian dog-days.

1. In *The Myth of Sisyphus*, London (Hamish Hamilton), 1955.

So much for the ambience of *The Outsider*. When we study its philosophy, the limpid style disguises a certain confusion. According to one critic, the Outsider himself represents the drying up of all bourgeois sources of sensation, and the complete decadence of renaissance man; he is a 'poor white'. According to another, Maurice Blanchot, he grows out of character in the last pages, when he becomes too articulate, and thus destroys the unity of the book. I don't agree with either. Meursault represents the neo-pagan, a reversion to Mediterranean man as once he was in Corinth or Carthage or Alexandria or Tarshish, as he is today in Casablanca or Southern California. He is sensual and well-meaning, profoundly in love with life, whose least pleasures, from a bathe to a yawn, afford him complete and silent gratification. He lives without anxiety in a continuous present and has no need to think or to express himself; there is no Nordic why-clause in his pact with nature. The misfortunes into which he is led by his lazy desire to please and by his stubborn truthfulness gradually force the felt but unspoken philosophy of his existence to emerge into the open, and finally to express itself in words. To understand this last outburst we must study Camus' attitude to death. In his essay on the Roman ruins of Djemila he makes clear how much he admires the fortitude of the pagan ending, even as he shares the sure-set pagan passion for life. 'What does eternity matter to me? To lose the touch of flowers and women's hands is the supreme separation.' In his long essay on suicide in *The Myth of Sisyphus* he introduces his conceptions of the Absurd. 'Everything which exalts life adds at the same time to its absurdity,' he says in *Summer in Algiers*, and comes to the conclusion in the *Myth* that 'the Man under Sentence of Death is freer than the suicide – than the man who takes his own life'. The Suicide is a coward, he is one who

8

abandons the struggle with fate; the Condemned Man, however, has the chance to rise above the society which has condemned him and by his courage and intellectual liberation to nullify it. The egotism of suicides with their farewells and resentments is sometimes grotesque, the dignity of a brave man on the Scaffold never. In his own words, 'The precise opposite of the suicide is the man who is condemned to death ... The God-like disponibility of the condemned man before whom the prison gates open one day just before dawn, his incredible disinterestedness about everything except the pure flame of life within him, here I am quite sure that Death and Absurdity are the principles which generate the only rational Liberty – that which a human being can experience with body and soul.'

Having said all this, I will leave the reader to form his judgement. The Bourgeois Machinery with its decaying Christian morality, and bureaucratic self-righteousness which condemns the Outsider just because he is so foreign to it, is typical of a European code of Justice applied to a non-European people. A few hundred miles farther south and 'a touch of the Sun' would have been readily recognized, no doubt, as a cause for acquittal, in the case of a white man accused of murdering a native, but part of the rigidity of the moribund French court is the pompous assumption that Algiers is France. On the other hand it is a failure of sensibility on the part of Camus that the other sufferer in his story, the Moorish girl whose lover beats her up and whose brother is killed when trying to avenge her, is totally forgotten. She too may have been 'privileged' to love life just as much, so may her murdered brother, for they too were 'foreigners' to the Colonial System, and a great deal besides. But the new paganism, I am afraid, is no kinder to women than the old.

Nevertheless something will have to happen soon and a

9

new creed of happiness, charity and justice be brought to men. *The Outsider* is only a stage. He is a negative destructive force who shows up the unreality of bourgeois ethics. It is not enough to love life, we must teach everyone else to love it, we must appreciate that happiness is consciousness, and consciousness is one, that all its manifestations are sacred, and it is from these newer schools of novelists and poets in all countries that one day we will learn it.

CYRIL CONNOLLY

PART ONE

I

MOTHER died today. Or, maybe, yesterday; I can't be sure. The telegram from the Home says: *Your mother passed away. Funeral tomorrow. Deep sympathy.* Which leaves the matter doubtful; it could have been yesterday.

The Home for Aged Persons is at Marengo, some fifty miles from Algiers. With the two-o'clock bus I should get there well before nightfall. Then I can spend the night there, keeping the usual vigil beside the body, and be back here by tomorrow evening. I have fixed up with my employer for two day's leave; obviously, under the circumstances, he couldn't refuse. Still, I had an idea he looked annoyed, and I said, without thinking: 'Sorry, sir, but it's not my fault, you know.'

Afterwards it struck me I needn't have said that. I had no reason to excuse myself; it was up to him to express his sympathy and so forth. Probably he will do so the day after tomorrow, when he sees me in black. For the present, it's almost as if Mother weren't really dead. The funeral will bring it home to one, put an official seal on it, so to speak. . . .

I took the two-o'clock bus. It was a blazing hot afternoon. I'd lunched, as usual, at Céleste's restaurant. Everyone was most kind, and Céleste said to me, 'There's no one like a mother.' When I left they came with me to the door. It was something of a rush, getting away, as at the last moment I had to call in at Emmanuel's place to borrow his black tie and mourning-band. He lost his uncle a few months ago.

I had to run to catch the bus. I suppose it was my hurrying like that, what with the glare off the road and from the sky, the reek of petrol and the jolts, that made me feel so drowsy. Anyhow, I slept most of the way. When I woke I was leaning up against a soldier; he grinned, and asked me if I'd come from a long way off, and I just nodded, to cut things short. I wasn't in a mood for talking.

The Home is a little over a mile from the village. I went there on foot. I asked to be allowed to see Mother at once, but the door-porter told me I must see the Warden first. He wasn't free, and I had to wait a bit. The porter chatted with me while I waited; then he led me to the office. The Warden was a very small man, with grey hair and a Legion of Honour rosette in his buttonhole. He gave me a long look with his watery blue eyes. Then we shook hands, and he held mine so long that I began to feel embarrassed. After that he consulted a register on his table, and said:

'Madame Meursault entered the Home three years ago. She had no private means and depended entirely on you.'

I had a feeling he was blaming me for something, and started to explain. But he cut me short.

'There's no need to excuse yourself, my boy. I've looked up the record and obviously you weren't in a position to see that she was properly cared for. She needed someone to be with her all the time, and young men in jobs like yours don't get too much pay. In any case she was much happier in the Home.'

I said: 'Yes, sir; I'm sure of that.'

Then he added: 'She had good friends here, you know, old folks like herself, and one gets on better with people of one's own generation. You're much too young, you couldn't have been much of a companion to her.'

That was so. When we lived together, Mother was always watching me, but we hardly ever talked. During her first few weeks at the Home she used to cry a good deal. But that was only because she hadn't settled down. After a month or two she'd have cried if she'd been told to leave the Home. Because this, too, would have been a wrench. That was why, during the last year, I seldom went to see her. Also, it would have meant losing my Sunday – not to mention the fag of going to the bus, getting my ticket, and spending two hours on the journey, each way.

The Warden went on talking, but I didn't pay much attention. Finally he said:

'Now, I suppose you'd like to see your mother?'

I rose without replying and he led the way to the door. As we were going down the stairs he explained:

'I've had the body moved to our little mortuary – so as not to upset the other old people, you understand. Every time there's a death here, they're in a nervous state for two or three days. Which means, of course, extra work and worry for our staff.'

We crossed a courtyard where there were a number of old men, talking amongst themselves in little groups. They fell silent as we came up with them. Then, behind our backs, the chattering began again. Their voices reminded me of parakeets in a cage, only the sound wasn't quite so shrill. The Warden stopped outside the entrance of a small, low building.

'So here I leave you, Monsieur Meursault. If you want me for anything, you'll find me in my office. We propose to have the funeral tomorrow morning. That will enable you to spend the night beside your mother's coffin, as no doubt you would wish to do. Just one more thing; I gathered from your mother's friends that she wished to be buried with the rites of the Church. I've made arrangements for this; but I thought I should let you know.'

I thanked him. So far as I knew, my mother, though not a professed atheist, had never given a thought to religion in her life.

I entered the mortuary. It was a bright, spotlessly clean room, with whitewashed walls and a big skylight. The furniture consisted of some chairs and trestles. Two of the latter stood open in the centre of the room and the coffin rested on them. The lid was in place, but the screws had been given only a few turns and their nickelled heads stuck out above the wood, which was stained dark walnut. An Arab woman, a nurse I supposed, was sitting beside the bier; she was wearing a blue smock and had a rather gaudy scarf wound round her hair.

Just then the porter came up behind me. He'd evidently been running, as he was a little out of breath.

'We put the lid on, but I was told to unscrew it when you came, so that you could see her.'

While he was going up to the coffin I told him not to trouble.

'Eh? What's that?' he exclaimed. 'You don't want me to . . . ?'

'No,' I said.

He put back the screwdriver in his pocket and stared at me. I realized then that I shouldn't have said 'No', and it made me rather embarrassed. After eyeing me for some moments he asked:

'Why not?' But he didn't sound reproachful; he simply wanted to know.

'Well, really I couldn't say,' I answered.

He began twiddling his white moustache; then, without looking at me, said gently:

'I understand.'

He was a pleasant-looking man, with blue eyes and ruddy cheeks. He drew up a chair for me near the coffin, and seated himself just behind. The nurse got up and moved towards the door. As she was going by the porter whispered in my ear:

'It's a tumour she has, poor thing.'

I looked at her more carefully and I noticed that she had a bandage round her head, just below her eyes. It lay quite flat across the bridge of her nose, and one saw hardly anything of her face except that strip of whiteness.

As soon as she had gone, the porter rose.

'Now I'll leave you to yourself.'

I don't know whether I made some gesture, but instead of going he halted behind my chair. The sensation of someone posted at my back made me uncomfortable. The sun was getting low and the whole room was flooded with a pleasant mellow light. Two hornets were buzzing overhead, against the skylight. I was so sleepy I could hardly keep my eyes open. Without looking round I asked the porter how long he'd been at the Home. 'Five years.' The answer came so pat that one could have thought he'd been expecting my question.

That started him off, and he became quite chatty. If anyone had told him ten years ago that he'd end his days as doorporter at a Home at Marengo, he'd never have believed it. He was sixty-four, he said, and hailed from Paris.

When he said that, I broke in without thinking, 'Ah, you don't come from here?'

I remembered then that, before taking me to the Warden, he'd told me something about Mother. He said she'd have to be buried mighty quickly because of the heat in these parts, especially down in the plain. 'At Paris they keep the body for three days, sometimes four.' After that he mentioned that he'd spent the best part of his life in Paris, and could never manage to forget it. 'Here', he said, 'things have to go with a rush, like. You've hardly time to get used to the idea that somebody's dead, before you're hauled off to the funeral.' 'That's enough,' his wife put in. 'You didn't ought to say such things to the poor young gentleman.' The old fellow blushed and began to apologize. I told him it was quite all right. As a matter of fact I found it rather interesting, what he'd been telling me; I hadn't thought of that before.

Now he went on to say that he'd entered the Home as an ordinary inmate. But he was still quite hale and hearty, so when the porter's job fell vacant, he offered to take it on.

I pointed out that, even so, he was really an inmate like the others, but he wouldn't hear of it. He was 'an official, like.' I'd been struck before that by his habit of saying 'they' or, less often, 'them old folks,' when referring to inmates no older than himself. Still, I could see his point of view. As door-porter he had a certain standing, and some authority over the rest of them.

Just then the nurse returned. Night had fallen very quickly; all of a sudden, it seemed, the sky went black above the skylight. The porter switched on the lamps, and I was almost blinded by the blaze of light.

He suggested I should go to the refectory for dinner, but I wasn't hungry. Then he proposed bringing me a mug of *café au lait*. As I am very fond of *café au lait* I said 'Thanks', and a few minutes later he came back with a tray. I drank the coffee, and then I wanted a cigarette. But I wasn't sure if I should smoke, under the circumstances – in Mother's presence. I thought it over; really it didn't seem to matter, so I offered the porter a cigarette and we both smoked.

After a while he started talking again.

'You know, your mother's friends will be coming soon, to keep vigil with you beside the body. We always have a "vigil" here, when anyone dies. I'd better go and get some chairs and a pot of black coffee.'

The glare from the white walls was making my eyes smart, and I asked him if he couldn't turn off one of the lamps. 'Nothing doing,' he said. They'd arranged the lights like that; either one had them all on or none at all. After that I didn't pay much more attention to him. He went away, brought some chairs and set them out round the coffin. On one he placed a coffee-pot and ten or a dozen cups. Then he sat down facing me, on the far side of Mother. The nurse was at the other end of the room, with her back to me. I couldn't see what she was doing, but by the way her arms moved I guessed that she was knitting. I was feeling very comfortable; the coffee had warmed me up, and through the open door came scents of flowers, and breaths of cool night air. I think I dozed off for a while.

I was awakened by an odd rustling in my ears. After having had my eyes closed, I had a feeling that the light had grown even stronger than before. There wasn't a trace of shadow anywhere, and every object, each curve or angle, scored its outline on one's eyes. The old people, Mother's friends, were coming in. I counted ten in all, gliding almost soundlessly through the bleak white glare. None of the chairs creaked when they sat down. Never in my life had I seen anyone so clearly as I saw these people; not a detail of their clothes or features escaped me. And yet I couldn't hear them, and it was hard to believe they really existed.

Nearly all the women wore aprons, and the strings drawn tight round their waists made their big stomachs bulge still more. I'd never yet noticed what big paunches old women usually have. Most of the men, however, were thin as rakes, and they all carried sticks. What struck me most about their faces was that one couldn't see their eyes, only a dull glow in a sort of nest of wrinkles.

On sitting down, they looked at me, and wagged their heads awkwardly, sucking their lips in between their tooth-less gums. I couldn't decide if they were greeting me and trying to say something, or if it was due to some infirmity of age. I inclined to think that they were greeting me, after their fashion, but it had a queer effect, seeing all those old

19

fellows grouped round the porter, solemnly eyeing me and dandling their heads from side to side. For a moment I had an absurd impression that they had come to sit in judgement on me.

A few minutes later one of the women started weeping. She was in the second row and I couldn't see her face because of another woman in front. At regular intervals she emitted a little choking sob; one had a feeling she would never stop. The others didn't seem to notice. They sat in silence, slumped in their chairs, staring at the coffin or at their walking-sticks or any other object just in front of them, and never took their eyes off it. And still the woman sobbed. I was rather surprised, as I didn't know who she was. I wanted her to stop crying, but dared not speak to her. After a while the porter bent towards her and whispered in her ear; but she merely shook her head, mumbled something I couldn't catch, and went on sobbing as steadily as before.

The porter got up and moved his chair beside mine. At first he kept silent; then, without looking at me, he explained.

'She was devoted to your mother. She says your mother was her only friend in the world, and now she's all alone.'

I had nothing to say, and the silence lasted quite a while. Presently the woman's sighs and sobs became less frequent, and, after blowing her nose and snuffling for some minutes, she, too, fell silent.

I'd ceased feeling sleepy, but I was very tired and my legs were aching badly. And now I realized that the silence of these people was telling on my nerves. The only sound was a rather queer one; it came at longish intervals, and at first I was puzzled by it. However, after listening attentively, I guessed what it was; the old men were sucking at the insides of their cheeks, and this caused the odd, wheezing noises that had mystified me. They were so much absorbed in their thoughts that they didn't know what they were up to. I even had an impression that the dead body in their midst meant nothing at all to them. But now I suspect that I was mistaken about this.

We all drank the coffee, which the porter handed round. After that, I can't remember much; somehow the night went by. I can recall only one moment; I had opened my eyes and I saw the old men sleeping hunched up on their chairs, with one exception. Resting his chin on his hands clasped round his stick, he was staring hard at me, as if he had been waiting for me to wake. Then I fell asleep again. I woke up after a bit, because the ache in my legs had developed into a sort of cramp.

There was a glimmer of dawn above the skylight. A minute or two later one of the old men woke up and coughed repeatedly. He spat into a big check handkerchief, and each time he spat it sounded as if he was retching. This woke the others, and the porter told them it was time to make a move. They all got up at once. Their faces were ashen-grey after the long, uneasy vigil. To my surprise each of them shook hands with me, as though this night together, in which we hadn't exchanged a word, had created a kind of intimacy between us.

I was quite done in. The porter took me to his room and I tidied myself up a bit. He gave me some more white coffee, and it seemed to do me good. When I went out the sun was up and the sky mottled red above the hills between Marengo and the sea. A morning breeze was blowing and it had a pleasant salty tang. There was the promise of a very fine day. I hadn't been in the country for ages, and I caught myself thinking what an agreeable walk I might have had, if it hadn't been for Mother.

As it was, I waited in the courtyard under a plane-tree. I sniffed the smells of the cool earth and found I wasn't sleepy any more. Then I thought of the other fellows in the office. At this hour they'd be getting up, preparing to go to work; for me this was always the worst hour of the day. I went on thinking, like this, for ten minutes or so; then the sound of a bell inside the building attracted my attention. I could see movements behind the windows; then all was calm again. The sun had risen a little higher and was beginning to warm my feet. The Porter came across the yard and said the Warden wished to see me. I went to his office and he got me to sign some document. I noticed that he was in black, with pin-stripe trousers. He picked up the telephone-receiver and looked at me.

'The undertaker's men arrived some moments ago, and they will be going to the mortuary to screw down the coffin. Shall I tell them to wait, for you to have a last glimpse of your mother?'

'No,' I said.

He spoke into the receiver, lowering his voice.

'That's all right, Figeac. Tell the men to go there now.'

He then informed me that he was going to attend the funeral, and I thanked him. Sitting down behind his desk, he crossed his short legs and leant back. Besides the nurse on duty, he told me, he and I would be the only mourners at the funeral. It was a rule of the Home that inmates shouldn't attend funerals, though there was no objection to letting some of them sit up beside the coffin, the night before.

'It's for their own sakes,' he explained, 'to spare their feelings. But in this particular instance I've given permission for an old friend of your mother to come with us. His name is Thomas Pérez.' The Warden smiled. 'It's a rather touching little story in its way. He and your mother had become almost inseparable. The other old people used to tease Pérez about having a "fiancée". "When are you going to marry her?" they'd ask. He'd turn it with a laugh.

It was a standing joke, in fact. So, you can guess, he feels very badly about your mother's death. I thought I couldn't decently refuse him permission to attend the funeral. But, on our medical officer's advice, I forbade him to sit up beside the body last night.'

For some time we stayed without speaking. Then the Warden got up and went to the window. Presently he said:

'Ah, there's the padre from Marengo. He's a bit ahead of time.'

He warned me that it would take us a good three-quarters of an hour, walking to the church, which was in the village. Then we went downstairs.

The priest was waiting just outside the mortuary door. With him were two acolytes, one of whom had a censer. The priest was stooping over him, adjusting the length of the silver chain on which it hung. When he saw us he straightened up and said a few words to me, addressing me as 'My son'. Then he led the way into the mortuary.

I noticed at once that four men in black were standing behind the coffin and the screws in the lid had now been driven home. At the same moment I heard the Warden remark that the hearse had arrived, and the priest started his prayers. Then everybody made a move. Holding a strip of black cloth, the four men approached the coffin, while the priest, the boys and myself filed out. A lady I hadn't seen before was standing by the door. 'This is Monsieur Meursault,' the Warden said to her. I didn't catch her name, but I gathered she was a nursing sister attached to the Home. When I was introduced, she bowed, without the trace of a smile on her long, gaunt face. We stood aside from the doorway to let the coffin by; then, following the bearers down a corridor, we came to the front entrance, where a hearse was waiting. Oblong, glossy, varnished black all over, it vaguely reminded me of the pen-trays in the office.

Beside the hearse stood a quaintly dressed little man, whose duty it was, I understood, to supervise the funeral, as a sort of master of ceremonies. Near him, looking constrained, almost bashful, was old M. Pérez, my mother's special friend. He wore a soft felt hat with a pudding-basin crown and a very wide brim – he whisked it off the moment the coffin emerged from the doorway – trousers that concertina'd on his shoes, a black tie much too small for his high white double-collar. Under a bulbous, pimply nose, his lips were trembling. But what caught my attention most was his ears; pendulous, scarlet ears that showed up like blobs of sealing-wax on the pallor of his cheeks and were framed in wisps of silky white hair.

The undertaker's factotum shepherded us to our places, with the priest in front of the hearse, and the four men in black on each side of it. The Warden and myself came next, and, bringing up the rear, old Pérez and the nurse.

The sky was already a blaze of light, and the air stoking up rapidly. I felt the first waves of heat lapping my back, and my dark suit made things worse. I couldn't imagine why we waited so long for getting under way. Old Pérez, who had put on his hat, took it off again. I had turned slightly in his direction and was looking at him when the Warden started telling me more about him. I remember his saying that old Pérez and my mother used often to have a longish stroll together in the cool of the evening; sometimes they went as far as the village, accompanied by a nurse, of course.

I looked at the countryside, at the long lines of cypresses sloping up towards the skyline and the hills, the hot red soil dappled with vivid green, and here and there a lonely house sharply outlined against the light – and I could understand Mother's feelings. Evenings in these parts must be a sort of mournful solace. Now, in the full glare of the morning sun, with everything shimmering in the heat-haze, there was something inhuman, discouraging, about this landscape.

At last we made a move. Only then I noticed that Pérez had a slight limp. The old chap steadily lost ground as the hearse gained speed. One of the men beside it, too, fell back and drew level with me. I was surprised to see how quickly the sun was climbing up the sky, and just then it struck me that for quite a while the air had been throbbing with the hum of insects and the rustle of grass warming up. Sweat was trickling down my face. As I had no hat I tried to fan myself with my handkerchief.

The undertaker's man turned to me and said something that I didn't catch. At the same time he wiped the crown of his head with a handkerchief that he held in his left hand, while with his right he tilted up his hat. I asked him what he'd said. He pointed upwards

'Sun's pretty bad today, ain't it?'

'Yes,' I said.

After a while he asked: 'Is it your mother were burying?'

'Yes,' I said again.

'What was her age?'

'Well, she was getting on.' As a matter of fact I didn't know exactly how old she was.

After that he kept silent. Looking back, I saw Pérez limping along some fifty yards behind. He was swinging his big felt hat at arm's length, trying to make the pace. I also had a look at the Warden. He was walking with carefully measured steps, economizing every gesture. Beads of perspiration glistened on his forehead, but he didn't wipe them off.

I had an impression that our little procession was moving slightly faster. Wherever I looked I saw the same sun-drenched countryside, and the sky was so dazzling that I dared not raise my eyes. Presently we struck a patch of freshly tarred road. A shimmer of heat played over it and one's feet squelched at each step, leaving bright black gashes. In front, the coachman's glossy black hat looked like a lump of the same sticky substance, poised above the hearse. It gave one a queer, dreamlike impression, that bluey-white glare overhead and all this blackness round one: the sleek black of the hearse, the dull black of the men's clothes and the silvery black gashes in the road. And then there were the smells, smells of hot leather and horse-dung from the hearse, veined with whiffs of incense-smoke. What with these and the hangover from a poor night's sleep, I found my eyes and thoughts growing blurred.

I looked back again. Pérez seemed very far away now, almost hidden by the heat-haze; then, abruptly, he disappeared altogether. After puzzling over it for a bit, I guessed that he had turned off the road into the fields. Then I noticed that there was a bend of the road a little way ahead. Obviously Pérez, who knew the district well, had taken a short cut, so as to catch us up. He rejoined us soon after we were round the bend; then began to lose ground again. He took another short cut and met us again farther on; in fact this happened several times during the next half-hour. But soon I lost interest in his movements; my temples were throbbing and I could hardly drag myself along.

After that everything went with a rush; and also with such precision and matter-of-factness that I remember hardly any details. Except that when we were on the outskirts of the village the nurse said something to me. Her voice took me by surprise, it didn't match her face at all; it was musical and slightly tremulous. What she said was: 'If one goes too slowly, there's the risk of a heat-stroke. But, if one goes too fast, one perspires, and the cold air in the church gives one a chill.' I saw her point; either way one was for it.

Some other memories of the funeral have stuck in my

mind. The old boy's face, for instance, when he caught us up for the last time, just outside the village. His eyes were streaming with tears, of exhaustion or distress, or both together. But because of the wrinkles they couldn't flow down. They spread out, criss-crossed, and formed a sort of glaze over the old, worn face.

And I can remember the look of the church, the villagers in the street, the red geraniums on the graves, Pérez's fainting-fit – he crumpled up like a rag doll – the tawny red earth pattering on Mother's coffin, the bits of white roots mixed up with it; then more people, voices, the wait outside a café for the bus, the rumble of the engine, and my little thrill of pleasure when we entered the first brightly lit streets of Algiers, and I pictured myself going straight to bed and sleeping twelve hours at a stretch.

2

ON waking I understood why my employer had looked rather glum when I asked for my two days off; it was a Saturday today. I hadn't thought of this at the time; it only struck me when I was getting out of bed. Obviously he had seen that it would mean my getting four days' holiday straight off, and one couldn't expect him to like that. Still, for one thing, it wasn't my fault if Mother was buried yesterday and not today; and then, again, I'd have had my Saturday and Sunday off in any case. But naturally this didn't prevent me from seeing my employer's point.

Getting up was an effort, as I'd been really exhausted by the previous day's experiences. While shaving, I wondered how to spend the morning, and decided that a swim would do me good. So I caught the tram that goes down to the harbour.

It was quite like old times; a lot of young people were in the swimming-pool, amongst them Marie Cardona who used to be a typist at the office. I was rather keen on her in those days, and I fancy she liked me too. But she was with us so short a time that nothing came of it.

While I was helping her to climb on to a raft, I let my hand stray over her breasts. Then she lay flat on the raft, while I trod water. After a moment she turned and looked at me. Her hair was over her eyes and she was laughing. I clambered up on to the raft, beside her. The air was pleasantly warm and, half jokingly, I let my head sink back upon her lap. She didn't seem to mind, so I let it stay there. I had the sky full in my eyes, all blue and gold, and I could feel Marie's stomach rising and falling gently under my head. We must have stayed a good half-hour on the raft, both of us half asleep. When the sun got too hot she dived off and I followed. I caught her up, put my arm round her waist, and we swam side by side. She was still laughing.

While we were drying ourselves on the edge of the swimming-pool she said: 'I'm browner than you.' I asked her if she'd come to the cinema with me that evening. She laughed again and said 'Yes', if I'd take her to the comic everybody was talking about, the one with Fernandel in it.

When we had dressed, she stared at my black tie and asked if I was in mourning. I explained that my mother had died. 'When?' she asked, and I said, 'Yesterday.' She made no remark, though I thought she shrank away a little. I was just going to explain to her that it wasn't my fault, but I checked myself, as I remembered having said the same thing to my employer, and realizing then it sounded rather foolish. Still, foolish or not – somehow one can't help feeling a bit guilty, I suppose, about things like that.

Anyhow, by the evening Marie had forgotten all about it. The film was funny in parts, but much of it downright stupid. She pressed her leg against mine while we were in the picture-house, and I was fondling her breast. Towards the end of the show I kissed her, but rather clumsily. Afterwards she came back with me to my place.

When I woke up Marie had gone. She'd told me her aunt expected her first thing in the morning. I remembered it was a Sunday, and that put me off; I've never cared for Sundays. So I turned my head and lazily sniffed the smell of brine that Marie's head had left on the pillow. I slept until ten. After that I stayed in bed until noon, smoking cigarettes. I decided not to lunch at Céleste's restaurant as I usually did; they'd be sure to pester me with questions, and I dislike being questioned. So I fried some eggs, and ate them off the pan. I did without bread as there wasn't any left, and I couldn't be bothered going down to buy it.

After lunch I felt at a loose end and roamed about the little flat. It suited us well enough when Mother was with me, but now I was by myself it was too large and I'd moved the dining-table into my bedroom. That was now the only room I used; it had all the furniture I needed; a brass bedstead, a dressing-table, some cane chairs whose seats had more or less caved in, a wardrobe with a tarnished mirror. The rest of the flat was never used, so I didn't trouble to look after it.

A bit later, for want of anything to do, I picked up an old newspaper that was lying on the floor and read it. There was an advertisement for Kruschen Salts and I cut it out and pasted it into an album where I keep things that amuse me in the papers. Then I washed my hands and, as a last resource, went out on to the balcony.

My bedroom overlooks the main street of our district. Though it was a fine afternoon the paving-blocks were black and glistening. What few people were about seemed in an absurd hurry. First of all there came a family going for their Sunday afternoon walk; two small boys in sailor suits, with short trousers hardly down to their knees, and looking rather uneasy in their Sunday best; then a little girl with a big pink bow and black patent-leather shoes. Behind them was their mother, an enormously fat woman in a brown silk dress, and their father, a dapper little man, whom I knew by sight. He had a straw hat, a walking-stick, and a butterfly tie. Seeing him beside his wife, I understood why people said he came of a good family and had married beneath him.

Next came a group of young fellows, the local 'bloods', with sleek oiled hair, red ties, coats cut very tight at the waist, braided pockets, and square-toed shoes. I guessed they were going to one of the big cinemas in the centre of the town. That was why they had started out so early and were hurrying to the tram-stop, laughing and talking at the top of their voices.

After they had passed the street gradually emptied. By this time all the matinées must have begun. Only a few shopkeepers and cats remained about. Above the sycamores bordering the road the sky was cloudless, but the light was soft. The tobacconist on the other side of the street brought a chair out on to the pavement in front of his door and sat astride it, resting his arms on the back. The trams which a few minutes before had been crowded were now almost empty. In the little café, Chez Pierrot, beside the tobacconist's, the waiter was sweeping up the sawdust in the empty restaurant. A typical Sunday afternoon . . .

I turned my chair round and seated myself like the tobacconist, as it was more comfortable that way. After smoking a couple of cigarettes I went back to the room, got a tablet of chocolate and returned to the window to eat it.

Soon after, the sky clouded over and I thought a summer storm was coming. However, the clouds gradually lifted. All the same they had left in the street a sort of threat of rain, which made it darker. I stayed watching the sky for quite a while.

At five there was a loud clanging of trams. They were coming from the stadium in our suburb where there had been a football match. Even the back platforms were crowded and people were standing on the steps. Then another tram brought back the teams. I knew they were the players by the little suitcase each man carried. They were bawling out their team-song, 'Keep the ball rolling, boys'. One of them looked up at me and shouted, 'We licked them!' I waved my hand and called back, 'Good work!' From now on there was a steady stream of private cars.

The sky had changed again; a reddish glow was spreading up beyond the housetops. As dusk set in the street grew more crowded. People were returning from their walks, and I noticed the dapper little man with the fat wife amongst the passers-by. Children were whimpering and trailing wearily after their parents. After some minutes the local cinemas disgorged their audiences. I noticed that the young fellows coming from them were taking longer strides and gesturing more vigorously than at ordinary times; doubtless the picture they'd been seeing was of the Wild West variety. Those who had been to the picture-houses in the middle of the town came a little later, and looked more sedate, though a few were still laughing. On the whole, however, they seemed languid and exhausted. Some of them remained loitering in the street under my window. A group of girls came by, walking arm in arm. The young men under my window swerved so as to brush against them, and shouted humorous remarks, which made the girls turn their heads and giggle. I recognized them as girls from my part of the

31

town, and two or three of them, whom I knew, looked up and waved to me.

Just then the street-lamps came on, all together, and they made the stars that were beginning to glimmer in the night sky paler still. I felt my eyes getting tired, what with the lights and all the movement I'd been watching in the street. There were little pools of brightness under the lamps, and now and then a tramcar passed, lighting up a girl's hair, or a smile, or a silver bangle.

Soon after this, as the trams became fewer and the sky showed velvety black above the trees and lamps, the street grew emptier, almost imperceptibly, until a time came when there was nobody to be seen and a cat, the first of the evening, crossed unhurrying the deserted street.

It struck me that I'd better see about some dinner. I had been leaning so long on the back of my chair, looking down, that my neck hurt when I straightened myself up. I went down, bought some bread and spaghetti, did my cooking and ate my meal standing. I'd intended to smoke another cigarette at my window, but the night had turned rather chilly and I decided against it. As I was coming back, after shutting the window, I glanced at the mirror and saw reflected in it a corner of my table with my spirit-lamp and some bits of bread beside it. I occurred to me that somehow I'd got through another Sunday, that Mother now was buried, and tomorrow I'd be going back to work as usual. Really, nothing in my life had changed.

3

I HAD a busy morning in the office. My employer was in a good humour. He even inquired if I wasn't too tired, and followed it up by asking what Mother's age was. I thought a bit, then answered, 'Round about sixty', as I didn't want to make a blunder. At which he looked relieved – why, I can't imagine – and seemed to think that closed the matter.

There was a pile of bills of lading waiting on my desk and I had to go through them all. Before leaving for lunch I washed my hands. I always enjoyed doing this at midday. In the evening it was less pleasant, as the roller-towel after being used by so many people was sopping wet. I once brought this to my employer's notice. It was regrettable, he agreed – but, to his mind, a mere detail. I left the office building a little later than usual, at half past twelve, with Emmanuel, who works in the Forwarding Department. Our building overlooks the sea, and we paused for a moment on the steps to look at the shipping in the harbour. The sun was scorching hot. Just then a big truck came up, with a din of chains and backfires from the engine, and Emmanuel suggested we should try to jump it. I started to run. The truck was well away, and we had to chase it for quite a distance. What with the heat and the noise from the engine, I felt half dazed. All I was conscious of was our mad rush along the water-front, amongst cranes and winches, with dark hulls of ships alongside and masts swaying in the offing. I was the first to catch up with the truck. I took a flying jump, landed safely, and helped Emmanuel to scramble in beside me. We were both of us out of breath and the bumps of the truck on the roughly laid cobbles made things worse. Emmanuel chuckled, and panted in my ear, 'We've made it!'

By the time we reached Céleste's restaurant we were dripping with sweat. Céleste was at his usual place beside the entrance, with his apron bulging on his paunch, his white moustache well to the fore. When he saw he was sympathetic and 'hoped I wasn't feeling too badly'. I said 'No', but I was extremely hungry. I ate very quickly and had some coffee, to finish up. Then I went to my place and took a short nap, as I'd drunk a glass of wine too many. When I woke I smoked a cigarette before getting off my bed. I was a bit late and had to run for the tram. The office was stifling, and I was kept hard at it all the afternoon. So it came as a relief when we closed down and I was strolling slowly along the wharves in the coolness. The sky was green, and it was pleasant to be out of doors after the stuffy office. However, I went straight home as I had to put some potatoes on to boil.

The hall was dark and, when I was starting up the stairs, I almost bumped into old Salamano, who lived on the same floor as I. As usual, he had his dog with him. For eight years the two had been inseparable. Salamano's spaniel is an ugly brute, afflicted with some skin disease – mange, I expect; anyhow it has lost all its hair and its body is covered with brown scabs. Perhaps through living in one small room, cooped up with his dog, Salamano has come to resemble it. His towy hair has gone very thin, and he has reddish blotches on his face. And the dog has developed something of its master's queer hunched-up gait; it always has its muzzle stretched far forward and its nose to the ground. But, oddly enough, though so much alike, they detest each other.

Twice a day at eleven and six, the old fellow takes his dog for a walk, and for eight years that walk has never varied. You can see them in the rue de Lyon, the dog pulling his master along as hard as he can, till finally the old chap misses a step and nearly falls. Then he beats his dog and calls it names. The dog cowers and lags behind, and it's his master's turn to drag him along. Presently the dog forgets, starts tugging at the leash again, gets another hiding and more abuse. Then they halt on the pavement, the pair of them, and glare at each other; the dog with terror and the man with hatred in his eyes. Every time they're out this happens. When the dog wants to stop at a lamp-post, the old boy won't let him, and drags him on, and the wretched spaniel leaves behind him a trail of little drops. But, if he does it in the room, it means another hiding.

It's been going on like this for eight years, and Céleste always says it's a 'crying shame', and something should be done about it; but really one can't be sure. When I met him in the hall, Salamano was bawling at his dog, calling him a bastard, a lousy mongrel, and so forth, and the dog was whining. I said, 'Good evening', but the old fellow took no notice and went on cursing. So I thought I'd ask him what the dog had done. Again, he didn't answer, but went on shouting, 'You bloody cur!' and the rest of it. I couldn't see very clearly, but he seemed to be fixing something on the dog's collar. I raised my voice a little. Without looking round, he mumbled in a sort of suppressed fury: 'He's always in the way, blast him!' Then he started up the stairs, but the dog tried to resist and flattened itself out on the floor, so he had to haul it up on the leash, step by step.

Just then the man who lives on my floor came in from the street. The general idea hereabouts is that he's a pimp. But if one asks him what his job is, he says he's a warehouse-man. One thing's sure: he isn't popular in our street. Still, he often has a word for me, and drops in sometimes for a short talk in my room, because I listen to him. As a matter of fact, I find what he says quite interesting. So, really, I've no reason for freezing him off. His name is Sintès: Raymond Sintès. He's short and thick-set, has a nose like a boxer's, and always dresses very sprucely. He, too, once said to me, referring to Salamano, that it was 'a bloody shame', and asked me if I wasn't disgusted by the way the old man served his dog. I answered: 'No.'

We went up the stairs together, Sintès and I, and when I was turning in at my door, he said:

'Look here! How about having some grub with me? I've a black-pudding and some wine.'

It struck me that this would save my having to cook my dinner, so I said, 'Thanks very much.'

He, too, has only one room, and a little kitchen without a window. I saw a pink-and-white plaster angel above his bed, and some photos of sporting champions and naked girls pinned to the opposite wall. The bed hadn't been made and the room was dirty. He began by lighting a paraffin lamp; then fumbled in his pocket and produced a rather grimy bandage which he wrapped round his right hand. I asked him what the trouble was. He told me he'd been having a rough house with a fellow who'd annoyed him.

'I'm not one who looks for trouble,' he explained, 'only I'm a bit short-tempered. That fellow said to me, challenging, like, "Come down off that tram, if you're a man," I says, "You keep quiet, I ain't done nothing to you." Then he said I hadn't any guts. Well, that settled it. I got down off the tram and I said to him, "You better keep your mouth shut, or I'll shut it for you" – "I'd like to see you try!" says he. Then I gave him one across the face and laid him out good and proper. After a bit I started to help him to get up, but all he did was to kick at me from where he lay. So I gave him one with my knee and a couple more swipes. He was bleeding like a pig when I'd done with him. I asked him if he'd had enough, and said, "Yes."'

36

Sintès was busy fixing his bandage while he talked, and I was sitting on the bed.

'So you see,' he said, 'it wasn't my fault; he was asking for it, wasn't he?"

I nodded, and he added:

'As a matter of fact, I rather want to ask your advice about something; it's connected with this business. You've knocked about the world a bit, and I dare say you can help me. And then I'll be your pal for life; I never forget anyone who does me a good turn.'

When I made no comment, he asked me if I'd like us to be pals. I replied that I had no objection, and that appeared to satisfy him. He got out the black-pudding, cooked it in a frying-pan, then laid the table, putting out two bottles of wine. While he was doing this he didn't speak.

We started dinner, and then he began telling me the whole story, hesitating a bit at first.

'There's a girl behind it – as usual. We slept together pretty regular. I was keeping her, as a matter of fact, and she cost me a tidy sum. That fellow I knocked down is her brother.'

Noticing that I said nothing, he added that he knew what the neighbours said about him, but it was a filthy lie. He had his principles like everybody else, and a job in a warehouse.

'Well,' he said, 'to go on with my story. . . . I found out one day that she was letting me down.' He gave her enough money to keep her going, without extravagance, though; he paid the rent of her room and twenty francs a day for food. 'Three hundred francs for rent, and six hundred for her grub, with a little present thrown in now and then, a pair of stockings or what not. Say, a thousand francs a month. But that wasn't enough for my fine lady; she was always grumbling that she couldn't make both ends meet

37

with what I gave. So one day I says to her, "Look here, why not get a job for a few hours a day? That'd make things easier for me, too. I bought you a new frock this month, I pay your rent and give you twenty francs a day. But you go and waste your money at the café with a pack of girls. You give them coffee and sugar. And of course the money comes out of my pocket. I treat you on the square, and that's how you pay me back." But she wouldn't hear of working, though she kept on saying she couldn't make do with what I gave her. And then one day I found out she was doing the dirty on me.'

He went on to explain that he'd discovered a lottery ticket in her bag, and, when he asked where the money'd come from to buy it, she wouldn't tell him. Then, another time he'd found a pawn-ticket for two bracelets which he'd never set eyes on before.

'So I knew there was dirty work going on, and I told her I'd have nothing more to do with her. But, first, I gave her a good hiding, and I told her some home-truths. I said that there was only one thing interested her and that was getting into bed with men whenever she'd the chance. And I warned her straight, "You'll be sorry one day, my girl, and wish you'd got me back. All the girls in the street, they're jealous of your luck in having me to keep you."'

He'd beaten her till the blood came. Before that he'd never beaten her. 'Well, not hard, anyhow; only affectionately, like. She'd howl a bit, and I had to shut the window. Then, of course, it ended as per usual. But this time I'm done with her. Only, to my mind, I ain't punished her enough. See what I mean?'

He explained that it was about this he wanted my advice. The lamp was smoking, and he stopped pacing up and down the room, to lower the wick. I just listened, without speaking. I'd had a whole bottle of wine to myself and my head was buzzing. As I'd used up my cigarettes I was smoking Raymond's. Some late trams passed, and the last noises of the street died off with them. Raymond went on talking. What bored him was that he had 'a sort of lech on her' as he called it. But he was quite determined to teach her a lesson.

His first idea, he said, had been to take her to a hotel, and then call in the special police. He'd persuade them to put her on the register as a 'common prostitute' and that would make her wild. Then he'd looked up some friends of his in the underworld, fellows who kept tarts for what they could make out of them, but they had practically nothing to suggest. Still, as he pointed out, that sort of thing should have been right up their street; what's the good of being in that line if you don't know how to treat a girl who's let you down? When he told them that, they suggested he should 'brand' her. But that wasn't what he wanted either. It would need a lot of thinking out. . . . But, first, he'd like to ask me something. Before he asked it, though, he'd like to have my opinion of the story he'd been telling, in a general way.

I said I hadn't any, but I'd found it interesting.

Did I think she really had done the dirty on him?

I had to admit it looked like that. Then he asked me if I didn't think she should be punished, and what I'd do if I were in his shoes. I told him one could never be quite sure how to act in such cases, but I quite understood his wanting her to suffer for it.

I drank some more wine, while Raymond lit another cigarette and began explaining what he proposed to do. He wanted to write her a letter, 'a real stinker, that'll get her on the raw', and at the same time make her repent of what she'd done. Then, when she came back, he'd go to bed with her and, just when she was 'properly primed up', he'd spit

39

in her face and throw her out of the room. I agreed it wasn't a bad plan; it would punish her all right.

But, Raymond told me, he didn't feel up to writing the kind of letter that was needed, and that was where I could help. When I didn't say anything, he asked me if I'd mind doing it right away, and I said, 'No', I'd have a shot at it.

He drank off a glass of wine and stood up. Then he pushed aside the plates and the bit of cold pudding that was left, to make room on the table. After carefully wiping the oilcloth, he got a sheet of squared paper from the drawer of his bedside table; after that, an envelope, a small red wooden penholder and a square inkpot with purple ink in it. The moment he mentioned the girl's name I knew she was a Moor.

I wrote the letter. I didn't take much trouble over it, but I wanted to satisfy Raymond, as I'd no reason not to satisfy him. Then I read out what I'd written. Puffing at his cigarette, he listened, nodding now and then. 'Read it again, please,' he said. He seemed delighted. 'That's the stuff,' he chuckled. 'I could tell you was a brainy sort, old boy, and you know what's what.'

At first I hardly noticed that 'old boy'. It came back to me when he slapped me on the shoulder and said, 'So now we're pals, ain't we?' I kept silence and he said it again. I didn't care one way or the other, but as he seemed so set on it, I nodded and said, 'Yes.'

He put the letter in the envelope and we finished off the wine. Then both of us smoked for some minutes, without speaking. The street was quite quiet, except when now and again a car passed. Finally I remarked that it was getting late, and Raymond agreed. 'Time's gone mighty fast this evening,' he added, and in a way that was true. I wanted to be in bed, only it was such an effort making a move. I must have looked tired, for Raymond told me 'one mustn't let things get one down.' At first I didn't catch his meaning. Then he explained that he had heard of my mother's death; anyhow, he said, that was something bound to happen one day or another. I appreciated that, and told him so.

When I rose Raymond shook hands very warmly, remarking that men always understood each other. After closing the door behind me I lingered for some moments on the landing. The whole building was quiet as the grave, a dank, dark smell rising from the well-hole of the stairs. I could hear nothing but the blood throbbing in my ears, and for a while I stood listening to it. Then the dog began to moan in old Salamano's room, and through the sleep-bound house the little plaintive sound rose slowly, like a flower growing out of the silence and the darkness.

4

I HAD a busy time in the office throughout the week. Raymond dropped in once to tell me he'd sent off the letter. I went to the pictures twice with Emmanuel, who doesn't always understand what's happening on the screen and asks one to explain it. Yesterday was Saturday, and Marie came as we'd arranged. She had a very pretty dress, with red and white stripes, and leather sandals, and I couldn't take my eyes off her. One could see the outline of her firm little breasts, and her sun-tanned face was like a velvety brown flower. We took the bus and went to a beach I know, some miles out of Algiers. It's just a strip of sand between two rocky spurs, with a line of rushes at the back, along the tide-line. At four o'clock the sun wasn't too hot, but the water was pleasantly tepid, and small, languid ripples were creeping up the sand.

Marie taught me a new game. The idea was, while one swam, to suck in the spray off the waves and, when one's mouth was full of foam, to lie on one's back and spout it out against the sky. It made a sort of frothy haze that melted into the air or fell back in a warm shower on one's cheeks. But very soon my mouth was smarting with all the salt I'd drawn in; then Marie came up and hugged me in the water, and pressed her mouth to mine. Her tongue cooled my lips, and we let the waves roll us about for a minute or two before swimming back to the beach.

When we had finished dressing, Marie looked hard at me. Her eyes were sparkling. I kissed her; after that neither of us spoke for quite a while. I pressed her to my side as we scrambled up the foreshore. Both of us were in a hurry to catch the bus, get back to my place, and tumble on to the bed. I'd left my window open and it was pleasant to feel the cool night air flowing over our sunburnt bodies.

Marie said she was free next morning so I proposed she should have lunch with me. She agreed, and I went down to buy some meat. On my way back I heard a woman's voice in Raymond's room. A little later old Salamano started grumbling at his dog and presently there was a sound of boots and paws on the wooden stairs; then, 'Filthy brute! Get on, you cur!' and the two of them went out into the street. I told Marie about the old chap's habits, and it made her laugh. She was wearing one of my pyjama suits, and had the sleeves rolled up. When she laughed I wanted her again. A moment later she asked me if I loved her. I said that sort of question had no meaning, really; but I supposed I didn't. She looked sad for a bit, but when we were getting our lunch ready she brightened up and started laughing, and when she laughs I always want to kiss her. It was just then that the row started in Raymond's room.

First we heard a woman saying something in a high-pitched voice; then Raymond bawling at her, 'You let me down, you bitch! I'll learn you to let me down!' There came some thuds, then a piercing scream – it made one's blood run cold – and in a moment there was a crowd of people on the landing. Marie and I went out to see. The woman was still screaming and Raymond still knocking her about. Marie said, wasn't it horrible! I didn't answer anything. Then she asked me to go and fetch a policeman, but I told her I didn't like policemen. However, one turned up presently; the lodger on the second floor, a plumber, came up with him. When he banged on the door the noise stopped inside the room. He knocked again and, after a moment, the woman started crying, and Raymond opened the door. He had a cigarette dangling from his underlip and a rather sickly smile, 'Your name?' Raymond gave his name. 'Take that cigarette out of your mouth when you're talking to me,' the policeman said gruffly. Raymond hesitated, glanced at me, and kept the cigarette in his mouth. The policeman promptly swung his arm and gave him a good hard smack on the left cheek. The cigarette shot from his lips and dropped a yard away. Raymond made a wry face, but said nothing for a moment. Then, in a humble tone he asked if he mightn't pick up his fag.

The officer said 'Yes,' and added: 'But don't you forget next time that we don't stand for any nonsense, not from blokes like you.'

Meanwhile the girl went on sobbing and repeating: 'He hit me, the coward. He's a pimp.'

'Excuse me, officer,' Raymond put in, 'but is that in order, calling a man a pimp in the presence of witnesses?'

The policeman told him to 'shut his trap'.

Raymond then turned to the girl. 'Don't you worry, my pet. We'll meet again.'

'That's enough,' the policeman said, and told the girl to go away. Raymond was to stay in his room till summoned to the police-station. 'You ought to be ashamed of yourself,' the policeman added, 'getting so tight you can't stand steady. Why, you're shaking all over!'

'I'm not tight,' Raymond explained. 'Only when I see you standing there and looking at me, I can't help trembling. That's only natural.'

Then he closed his door, and we all went away. Marie and I finished getting our lunch ready. But she hadn't any appetite, and I ate nearly all. She left at one, and then I had a nap.

Towards three there was a knock at my door and Raymond came in. He sat down on the edge of my bed and for a minute or two said nothing. I asked him how it had gone off. He said it had all gone quite smoothly at first, as per programme; only then she'd slapped his face and he'd seen red, and started thrashing her. As for what happened after that, he needn't tell me, as I was there.

'Well,' I said, 'you taught her a lesson all right, and that's what you wanted, isn't it?'

He agreed, and pointed out that whatever the police did, that wouldn't change the fact she'd had her punishment. As for the police, he knew exactly how to handle them. But he'd like to know if I'd expected him to return the blow when the policeman hit him.

I told him I hadn't expected anything whatsoever and, anyhow, I had no use for the police. Raymond seemed pleased and asked if I'd like to come out for a stroll with him. I got up from the bed and started brushing my hair. Then Raymond said that what he really wanted was for me to act as his witness. I told him I had no objection; only I didn't know what he expected me to say.

'It's quite simple,' he replied. 'You've only got to tell them that the girl had let me down.'

So I agreed to be his witness.

We went out together and Raymond stood me a brandy in a café. Then we had a game of billiards; it was a close game and I lost by only a few points. After that he proposed going to a brothel, but I refused; I didn't feel like it. As we were walking slowly back he told me how pleased he was at having paid out his mistress so satisfactorily. He made himself extremely amiable to me and I quite enjoyed our walk. When we were nearly home I saw old Salamano on the doorstep; he seemed very excited. I noticed that his dog wasn't with him. He was turning like a teetotum, looking in all directions, and sometimes peering into the darkness of the hall with his little bloodshot eyes. Then he'd mutter something to himself and start gazing up and down the street again.

Raymond asked him what was wrong, but he didn't answer at once. Then I heard him grunt, 'The bastard! The filthy cur!' When I asked him where his dog was, he scowled at me and snapped out, 'Gone!' A moment later, all of a sudden, he launched out into it.

'I'd taken him to the Parade Ground as usual. There was a fair on, and one could hardly move for the crowd. I stopped at one of the booths to look at the Handcuff King. When I turned to go, the dog was gone. I'd been meaning to get a smaller collar, but I never thought the brute could slip it and get away like that.'

Raymond assured him the dog would find its way home, and told him stories of dogs that had travelled miles and miles to get back to their masters. But this seemed to make the old fellow even more worried than before.

'Don't you understand, they'll do away with him; the police, I mean. It's not likely anyone will take him in and look after him; with all those scabs he puts everybody off.'

I told him that there was a pound at the police station, where stray dogs are taken. His dog was certain to be there, and he could get it back on payment of a small charge. He asked me how much the charge was, but there I couldn't help him. Then he flew into a rage again.

'Is it likely I'd give money for a tyke like that? No bloody fear! They can kill him for all I care.' And he went on calling his dog the usual names.

Raymond gave a laugh and turned into the hall. I followed him upstairs and we parted on the landing. A minute or two later I heard Salamano's footsteps and a knock on my door.

When I opened it, he halted for a moment in the doorway.

'Excuse me . . . I hope I'm not disturbing you.'

I asked him in, but he shook his head. He was staring at his toe-caps, and the gnarled old hands were trembling. Without meeting my eyes, he started talking.

'They won't really take him from me, will they, Monsieur Meursault? Surely they wouldn't do a thing like that. If they do – I don't know what will become of me.'

I told him that, so far as I knew, they kept stray dogs in the pound for three days, waiting for their owners to call for them. After that they disposed of the dogs as they thought fit.

He stared at me in silence for a moment, then said, 'Good evening.' After that I heard him pacing up and down his room for quite a while. Then his bed creaked. Through the wall there came to me a little wheezing sound, and I guessed that he was weeping. For some reason, I don't know what, I began thinking of Mother. But I had to get up early next day; so, as I wasn't feeling hungry, I did without supper, and went straight to bed.

5

RAYMOND rang me up at the office. He said that a friend of his – to whom he'd spoken about me – invited me to spend next Sunday at his little seaside bungalow just outside Algiers. I told him I'd have been delighted; only I had promised to spend Sunday with a girl. Raymond promptly replied that she could come, too. In fact, his friend's wife would be very pleased not to be the only woman in a party of men.

I'd have liked to hang up at once, as my employer doesn't approve of one's using the office phone for private calls. But Raymond asked me to hold on; he had something else to tell me, and that was why he'd rung me up, though he could have waited till the evening to pass on the invitation.

'It's like this,' he said. 'I've been shadowed all the morning by some Arabs. One of them's the brother of that girl I had the row with. If you see him hanging round the house when you come back, pass me the word.'

I promised to do so.

Just then, my employer sent for me. For a moment I felt uneasy as I expected he was going to tell me to stick to my work and not waste time chattering with friends over the phone. However, it was nothing of the kind. He wanted to discuss a project he had in view, though so far he'd come to no decision. It was to open a branch at Paris, so as to be able to deal with the big companies on the spot, without postal delays, and he wanted to know if I'd like a post there.

'You're a young man,' he said, 'and I'm pretty sure you'd enjoy living in Paris. And, of course, you could travel about France for some months in the year.'

I told him I was quite prepared to go; but really I didn't care much one way or the other.

He then asked if a 'change of life', as he called it, didn't appeal to me, and I answered that one never changed one's real life; anyhow, one life was as good as another and my present one suited me quite well.

At this he looked rather hurt, and told me that I always shilly-shallied, and that I lacked ambition – a grave defect, to his mind, when one was in business.

I returned to my work. I'd have preferred not to vex him, but I saw no reason for 'changing my life'. By and large it wasn't an unpleasant one. As a student I'd had plenty of ambition of the kind he meant. But, when I had to drop my studies, I very soon realized all that was pretty futile.

Marie came that evening and asked me if I'd marry her. I said I didn't mind; if she was keen on it, we'd get married.

Then she asked me again if I loved her. I replied, much as before, that her question meant nothing or next to nothing – but I supposed I didn't.

'If that's how you feel,' she said, 'why marry me?'

I explained that it had no importance really but, if it would give her pleasure, we could get married right away. I pointed out that anyhow the suggestion came from her; as for me, I'd merely said 'Yes.'

Then she remarked that marriage was a serious matter. To which I answered: 'No.'

She kept silent after that, staring at me in a curious way. Then she asked:

'Suppose another girl had asked you to marry her – I mean, a girl you liked in the same way as you like me – would you have said "Yes" to her, too?'

'Naturally.'

Then she said she wondered if she really loved me or not. I, of course, couldn't enlighten her as to that. And, after

48

another silence, she murmured something about my being 'a queer fellow'. 'And I dare say that's why I love you,' she added. 'But maybe that's why one day I'll come to hate you.'

To which I had nothing to say, so I said nothing.

She thought for a bit, then started smiling, and, taking my arm, repeated that she was in earnest; she really wanted to marry me.

'All right,' I answered. 'We'll get married whenever you like.' I then mentioned the proposal made by my employer and Marie said she'd love to go to Paris.

When I told her I'd lived in Paris for a while, she asked me what it was like.

'A dingy sort of town, to my mind. Masses of pigeons and dark courtyards. And the people have washed-out, white faces.'

Then we went for a walk all the way across the town by the main streets. The women were good-lookers, and I asked Marie if she, too, noticed this. She said 'Yes' and that she saw what I meant. After that we said nothing for some minutes. However, as I didn't want her to leave me, I suggested we should dine together at Céleste's. She'd have loved to dine with me, she said, only she was booked up for the evening. We were near my place, and I said, 'Au revoir, then.'

She looked me in the eyes.

'Don't you want to know what I'm doing this evening?'

I did want to know, but I hadn't thought of asking her, and I guessed she was making a grievance of it. I must have looked embarrassed, for suddenly she started laughing and bent towards me, pouting her lips for a kiss.

I went by myself to Céleste's. When I had just started my dinner an odd-looking little woman came in and asked if she might sit at my table. Of course she might. She had a chubby face like a ripe apple, bright eyes, and moved in a curiously jerky way as if she were on wires. After taking off her close-fitting jacket she sat down and started studying the bill of fare with a sort of rapt attention. Then she called Céleste and gave her order, very fast but quite distinctly; one didn't lose a word. While waiting for the *hors d'œuvre* she opened her bag, took out a slip of paper and a pencil, and added up the bill in advance. Diving into her bag again, she produced a purse and took from it the exact sum plus a small tip, and placed it on the cloth in front of her.

Just then the waiter brought the *hors d'œuvre*, which she proceeded to wolf down voraciously. While waiting for the next course, she produced another pencil, this time a blue one, from her bag, and the radio magazine for the coming week, and started making ticks against almost all the items of the daily programmes. There were a dozen pages in the magazine and she continued studying them closely throughout the meal. When I'd finished mine she was still ticking off items with the same meticulous attention. Then she rose, put on her jacket again with the same abrupt, robot-like gestures, and walked briskly out of the restaurant.

Having nothing better to do, I followed her for a short distance. Keeping on the kerb of the pavement, she walked straight ahead, never swerving or looking back, and it was extraordinary how fast she covered the ground, considering her smallness. In fact, the pace was too much for me, and I soon lost sight of her and turned back homewards. For a moment the 'little robot' (as I thought of her) had much impressed me, but I soon forgot about her.

As I was turning in at my door I ran into old Salamano. I asked him into my room, and he informed me that his dog was definitely lost. He'd been to the pound to inquire, but it wasn't there, and the staff told him it had probably been run over. When he asked them whether it was any use inquiring about it at the police station, they said the police had more important things to attend to than keeping records of stray dogs run over in the streets. I suggested he should get another dog, but, reasonably enough, he pointed out that he'd become used to this one, and it wouldn't be the same thing.

I was seated on my bed, with my legs up, and Salamano on a chair beside the table, facing me, his hands spread on his knees. He had kept on his battered felt hat and was mumbling away behind his draggled yellowish moustache. I found him rather boring, but I had nothing to do and didn't feel sleepy. So, to keep the conversation going, I asked some questions about his dog – how long he had had it and so forth. He told me he had got it soon after his wife's death. He'd married rather late in life. When a young man, he'd wanted to go on the stage; during his military service he'd often played in the regimental theatricals and acted rather well, so everybody said. However, finally, he had taken a job in the railway, and he didn't regret it, as now he had a small pension. He and his wife had never hit it off very well, but they'd got used to each other, and when she died he felt lonely. One of his mates on the railway whose bitch had just had pups, had offered him one, and he had taken it, as a companion. He'd had to feed it from the bottle at first. But, as a dog's life is shorter than a man's, they'd so to speak grown old together.

'He was a cantankerous brute,' Salamano said. 'Now and then we had some proper set-tos, he and I. But he was a good tyke all the same.'

I said he looked well bred, and that evidently pleased the old man.

'Ah, but you should have seen him before his illness!' he said. 'He had a wonderful coat; in fact, that was his best point really. I tried hard to cure him; every mortal night after he got that skin disease I rubbed an ointment in. But his real trouble was old age, and there's no curing that.'

Just then I yawned, and the old chap said he'd better make a move. I told him he could stay, and that I was sorry about what had happened to his dog. He thanked me, and mentioned that my mother had been fond of his dog. He referred to her as 'your poor mother', and was afraid I must be feeling her death terribly. When I said nothing he added hastily and with a rather embarrassed air that some of the people in the street said nasty things about me because I'd sent my mother to the Home. But he, of course, knew better; he knew how devoted to my mother I had always been.

I answered – why, I still don't know – that it surprised me to learn I'd produced such a bad impression. As I couldn't afford to keep her here, it seemed the obvious thing to do, to send her to a Home. 'In any case,' I added, 'for years she'd never had a word to say to me, and I could see she was moping, with no one to talk to.'

'Yes,' he said, 'and at a Home one makes friends, anyhow.'

He got up, saying it was high time for him to be in bed, and added that life was going to be a bit of a problem for him, under the new conditions. For the first time since I'd known him he held out his hand to me – rather shyly, I thought – and I could feel the scales on his skin. Just as he was going out of the door, he turned and, smiling a little, said:

'Let's hope the dogs won't bark again tonight. I always think it's mine I hear. . . .'

6

I⊤ was an effort waking up that Sunday morning; Marie
had to jog my shoulders and shout my name. As we wanted
to get into the water early, we didn't trouble about break-
fast. My head was aching slightly and my first cigarette had
a bitter taste. Marie told me I looked like a mourner at a
funeral, and I certainly did feel very limp. She was wearing
a white dress and had her hair loose. I told her she looked
quite ravishing like that, and she laughed happily.

On our way out we banged on Raymond's door, and he
shouted that he'd be with us in a jiffy. We went down to
the street and, because of my being rather under the weather
and our having kept the blind down in my room, the glare
of the morning sun hit me in the eyes like a clenched fist.

Marie, however, was almost dancing with delight, and
kept repeating, 'What a heavenly day!' After a few minutes
I was feeling better, and noticed that I was hungry. I mentioned this to Marie but she paid no attention. She was
carrying an oilcloth bag in which she had stowed our bathing
kit and a towel. Presently we heard Raymond shutting his
door. He was wearing blue trousers, a short-sleeved
white shirt, and a straw hat. I noticed that his forearms were
rather hairy, but the skin was very white beneath. The
straw hat made Marie giggle. Personally, I was rather put
off by his get-up. He seemed in high spirits and was whistling
as he came down the stairs. He greeted me with, 'Hullo, old
boy!' and addressed Marie as 'Mademoiselle'.

On the previous evening we had visited the police station,
where I gave evidence for Raymond – about the girl's
having been false to him. So they let him off with a warning.
They didn't check my statement.

After some talk on the doorstep we decided to take the bus. The beach was within easy walking distance, but the sooner we got there the better. Just as we were starting for the bus stop, Raymond plucked my sleeve and told me to look across the street. I saw some Arabs lounging against the tobacconist's window. They were staring at us silently, in the special way these people have – as if we were blocks of stone or dead trees. Raymond whispered that the second Arab from the left was 'his man', and I thought he looked rather worried. However, he assured me that all that was ancient history. Marie, who hadn't followed his remarks, asked, 'What is it?'

I explained that those Arabs across the way had a grudge against Raymond. She insisted on our going at once. Then Raymond laughed, and squared his shoulders. The young lady was quite right, he said. There was no point in hanging about here. Half-way to the bus stop he glanced back over his shoulder and said the Arabs weren't following. I, too, looked back. They were exactly as before, gazing in the same vague way at the spot where we had been.

When we were in the bus, Raymond, who now seemed quite at ease, kept making jokes to amuse Marie. I could see he was attracted by her, but she had hardly a word for him. Now and again she would catch my eye and smile.

We alighted just outside Algiers. The beach is not far from the bus stop; one has only to cross a patch of high land, a sort of plateau, which overlooks the sea and shelves down steeply to the sands. The ground here was covered with yellowish pebbles and wild lilies that showed snow-white against the blue of the sky, which had already the hard metallic glint it gets on very hot days. Marie amused herself swishing her bag against the flowers and sending the petals showering in all directions. Then we walked between two rows of little houses with wooden balconies and green or white palings. Some of them were half-hidden in clumps of tamarisks; others rose naked from the stony plateau. Before we came to the end of it, the sea was in full view; it lay smooth as a mirror, and in the distance a big headland jutted out over its black reflection. Through the still air came the faint buzz of a motor-engine and we saw a fishing-boat very far out, gliding almost imperceptibly across the dazzling smoothness.

Marie picked some rock-irises. Going down the steep path leading to the sea, we saw some bathers already on the sands.

Raymond's friend owned a small wooden bungalow at the near end of the beach. Its back rested against the cliff-side, while the front stood on piles, which the water was already lapping. Raymond introduced us to his friend, whose name was Masson. He was tall, broad-shouldered and thick-set; his wife was a plump, cheerful little woman, who spoke with a Paris accent.

Masson promptly told us to make ourselves at home. He had gone out fishing, he said, first thing in the morning, and there would be fried fish for lunch. I congratulated him on his little bungalow, and he said he always spent his week-ends and holidays here. 'With the missus, needless to say,' he added. I glanced at her, and noticed that she and Marie seemed to be getting on well together; laughing and chattering away. For the first time, perhaps, I seriously considered the possibility of my marrying her.

Masson wanted to have a swim at once, but his wife and Raymond were disinclined to move. So only the three of us, Marie, Masson, and myself, went down to the beach. Marie promptly plunged in, but Masson and I waited for a bit. He was rather slow of speech and had, I noticed, a habit of saying 'and what's more' between his phrases – even when the second added nothing really to the first. Talking of Marie, he said: 'She's an awfully pretty girl, and, what's more, charming.'

But I soon ceased paying attention to this trick of his; I was basking in the sunlight which, I noticed, was making me feel much better. The sand was beginning to stoke up under-foot and, though I was eager for a dip, I postponed it for a minute or two more. At last I said to Masson: 'Shall we go in now?' and plunged. Masson walked in gingerly and only began to swim when he was out of his depth. He swam hand over hand and made slow headway, so I left him behind and caught up Marie. The water was cold and I felt all the better for it. We swam a long way out, Marie and I side by side, and it was pleasant feeling how our movements matched, hers and mine, and how we were both in the same mood, enjoying every moment.

Once we were out in the open, we lay on our backs and, as I gazed up at the sky, I could feel the sun drawing up the film of salt water on my lips and cheeks. We saw Masson swim back to the beach and slump down on the sand under the sun. In the distance he looked enormous, like a stranded whale. Then Marie proposed that we should swim tandem. She went ahead and I put my arms round her waist from behind, and while she drew me forward with her arm-strokes, I kicked out behind to help us on.

That sound of little splashes had been in my ears for so long that I began to feel I'd had enough of it. So I let go of Marie and swam back at an easy pace, taking long, deep breaths. When I made the beach I stretched myself belly-downwards beside Masson, resting my face on the sand. I told him 'it was fine' here and he agreed. Presently Marie came back. I raised my head to watch her approach. She was glistening with brine and holding her hair back. Then she lay down beside me and what with the combined warmth of our bodies and the sun, I felt myself dropping off to sleep.

After a while Marie tugged my arm and said Masson had gone to his place; it must be nearly lunch-time. I rose at once, as I was feeling hungry, but Marie told me I hadn't kissed her once since the early morning. That was so – though I'd wanted to, several times. 'Let's go into the water again,' she said, and we ran into the sea and lay flat amongst the ripples for a moment. Then we swam a few strokes and when we were almost out of our depth she flung her arms round me and hugged me. I felt her legs twining round mine, and my senses tingled.

When we got back, Masson was on the steps of his bungalow, shouting to us to come. I told him I was ravenously hungry, and he promptly turned to his wife and said he'd taken quite a fancy to me. The bread was excellent, and I had my full share of the fish. Then came some steak and chips. None of us spoke while eating. Masson drank a lot of wine and kept refilling my glass the moment it was empty. By the time coffee was handed round I was feeling slightly muzzy, and I started smoking one cigarette after another. Masson, Raymond, and I discussed a plan of spending the whole of August on the beach together, sharing expenses.

Suddenly Marie exclaimed: 'I say! Do you know the time? It's only half past eleven!'

We were all surprised at that, and Masson remarked that we'd had a very early lunch, but really lunch was a movable feast, one had it when one felt like it.

This set Marie laughing, I don't know why. I suspect she'd drunk a bit too much.

Then Masson asked if I'd like to come with him for a stroll on the beach.

'My wife always has a nap after lunch,' he said. 'Personally

I find it doesn't agree with me; what I need is a short walk. I'm always telling her it's much better for the health. But of course she's entitled to her own opinion.'

Marie proposed to stay and help with the washing-up. Mme Masson smiled and said that, in that case, the first thing was to get the men out of the way. So we went out together, the three of us.

The light was almost vertical and the glare from the water seared one's eyes. The beach was quite deserted now. One could hear a faint tinkle of knives and forks and crockery in the shacks and bungalows lining the foreshore. Heat was welling up from the rocks and one could hardly breathe.

At first Raymond and Masson talked of things and people I didn't know. I gathered that they'd been acquainted for some time and had even lived together for a while. We went down to the water's edge and walked along it; now and then a longer wave wetted our canvas shoes. I wasn't thinking of anything, as all that sunlight beating down on my bare head made me feel half asleep.

Just then Raymond said something to Masson that I didn't quite catch. But at the same moment I noticed two Arabs in blue dungarees a long way down the beach, coming in our direction. I gave Raymond a look and he nodded, saying, 'That's him.' We walked steadily on. Masson wondered how they'd managed to track us here. My impression was that they had seen us taking the bus and noticed Marie's oilcloth bathing-bag; but I didn't say anything.

Though the Arabs walked quite slowly they were much nearer already. We didn't change our pace, but Raymond said:

'Listen! If there's a rough house, you, Masson, take on the second one. I'll tackle the fellow who's after me. And you, Meursault, stand by to help if another one comes up, and lay him out.'

I said, 'Right', and Masson put his hands in his pockets.

The sand was hot as fire and I could have sworn it was glowing red. The distance between us and the Arabs was steadily decreasing. When we were only a few steps away the Arabs halted. Masson and I slowed down, while Raymond went straight up to his man. I couldn't hear what he said, but I saw the native lowering his head, as if to butt him in the chest. Raymond lashed out promptly and shouted to Masson to come. Masson went up to the man he had been marking and struck him twice with all his might. The fellow fell flat into the water and stayed there some seconds with bubbles coming up to the surface round his head. Meanwhile Raymond had been slogging the other man, whose face was streaming with blood. He glanced at me over his shoulder and shouted:

'Just you watch! I ain't finished with him yet!'

'Look out!' I cried. 'He's got a knife.'

I spoke too late. The man had gashed Raymond's arm and his mouth as well.

Masson sprang forward. The other Arab got up from the water and placed himself behind the fellow with the knife. We didn't dare to move. The two natives backed away slowly, keeping us at bay with the knife and never taking their eyes off us. When they were at a safe distance they swung round and took to their heels. We stood stock still, with the sunlight beating down on us. Blood was dripping from Raymond's wounded arm, which he was squeezing hard above the elbow.

Masson remarked that there was a doctor who always spent his Sundays here, and Raymond said: 'Good. Let's go to him at once.' He could hardly get the words out as the blood from his other wound made bubbles in his mouth.

We each gave him an arm and helped him back to the bungalow. Once we were there he told us the wounds weren't so very deep and he could walk to where the doctor was. Marie had gone quite pale, and Mme Masson was in tears.

Masson and Raymond went off to the doctor's while I was left behind at the bungalow to explain matters to the women. I didn't much relish the task and soon dried up and started smoking, staring at the sea.

Raymond came back at about half past one, accompanied by Masson. He had his arm bandaged and a strip of sticking-plaster on the corner of his mouth. The doctor assured him it was nothing serious, but he was looking very glum. Masson tried to make him laugh, but without success.

Presently Raymond said he was going for a stroll on the beach. I asked him where he proposed to go and he mumbled something about 'wanting to take the air'. We – Masson and I – then said we'd go with him, but he flew into a rage and told us to mind our own business. Masson said we mustn't insist, seeing the state he was in. However, when he went out, I followed him.

It was like a furnace outside, with the sunlight splintering into flakes of fire on the sand and sea. We walked for quite a while, and I had an idea that Raymond had a definite idea where he was going; but probably I was mistaken about this.

At the end of the beach we came to a small stream that had cut a channel in the sand, after coming out from behind a biggish rock. There we found our two Arabs again, lying on the sand in their blue dungarees. They looked harmless enough, as if they didn't bear any malice, and neither made any move when we approached. The man who had slashed Raymond stared at him without speaking. The other man was blowing down a little reed and extracting from it three notes of the scale, which he played over and over again, while he watched us from the corner of an eye.

For a while nobody moved; it was all sunlight and silence except for the tinkle of the stream and those three little lonely sounds. Then Raymond put his hand to his revolver-pocket, but the Arabs still didn't move. I noticed that the man playing on the reed had his big toes splayed out almost at right angles to his feet.

Still keeping his eyes on his man, Raymond said to me: 'Shall I plug him one?'

I thought quickly. If I told him not to, considering the mood he was in, he might very well fly into a temper and use his gun. So I said the first thing that came into my head.

'He hasn't spoken to you yet. It would be a low-down trick to shoot him like that, in cold blood.'

Again, for some moments one heard nothing but the tinkle of the stream and the flute-notes weaving through the hot, still air.

'Well,' Raymond said at last, 'if that's how you feel, I'd better say something insulting, and if he answers back I'll loose off.'

'Right,' I said. 'Only, if he doesn't get out his knife you've no business to fire.'

Raymond was beginning to fidget. The Arab with the reed went on playing, and both of them watched all our movements.

'Listen,' I said to Raymond. 'You take on the fellow on the right, and give me your revolver. If the other one starts making trouble or gets out his knife, I'll shoot.'

The sun glinted on Raymond's revolver as he handed it to me. But nobody made a move yet; it was just as if everything had closed in on us so that we couldn't stir. We could only watch each other, never lowering our eyes; the whole world seemed to have come to a standstill on this little strip of sand between the sunlight and the sea, the twofold silence of the reed and stream. And just then it crossed my mind that one might fire, or not fire – and it would come to absolutely the same thing.

Then, all of a sudden, the Arabs vanished; they'd slipped like lizards under cover of the rock. So Raymond and I turned and walked back. He seemed happier, and began talking about the bus to catch for our return.

When we reached the bungalow Raymond promptly went up the wooden steps, but I halted on the bottom one. The light seemed thudding in my head and I couldn't face the effort needed to go up the steps and make myself amiable to the women. But the heat was so great that it was just as bad staying where I was, under that flood of blinding light falling from the sky. To stay, or to make a move – it came to much the same. After a moment I returned to the beach, and started walking.

There was the same red glare as far as the eye could reach, and small waves were lapping the hot sand in little, flurried gasps. As I slowly walked towards the boulders at the end of the beach I could feel my temples swelling under the impact of the light. It pressed itself upon me, trying to check my progress. And each time I felt a hot blast strike my forehead, I gritted my teeth, I clenched my fists in my trouser-pockets and keyed up every nerve to fend off the sun and the dark befuddlement it was pouring into me. Whenever a blade of vivid light shot upwards from a bit of shell or broken glass lying on the sand, my jaws set hard. I wasn't going to be beaten, and I walked steadily on.

The small black hump of rock came into view far down the beach. It was rimmed by a dazzling sheen of light and feathery spray, but I was thinking of the cold, clear stream behind it, and longing to hear again the tinkle of running water. Anything to be rid of the glare, the sight of women in tears, the strain and effort – and to retrieve the pool of shadow by the rock and its cool silence!

But when I came nearer I saw that Raymond's Arab had returned. He was by himself this time, lying on his back, his hands behind his head, his face shaded by the rock while the sun beat on the rest of his body. One could see his dungarees steaming in the heat. I was rather taken aback; my impression had been that the incident was closed, and I hadn't given a thought to it on my way here.

On seeing me the Arab raised himself a little, and his hand went to his pocket. Naturally, I gripped Raymond's revolver in the pocket of my coat. Then the Arab let himself sink back again, but without taking his hand from his pocket. I was some distance off, at least ten yards, and most of the time I saw him as a blurred dark form wobbling in the heat-haze. Sometimes, however, I had glimpses of his eyes glowing between the half-closed lids. The sound of the waves was even lazier, feebler, than at noon. But the light hadn't changed; it was pounding fiercely as ever on the long stretch of sand that ended at the rock. For two hours the sun seemed to have made no progress; becalmed in a sea of molten steel. Far out on the horizon a steamer was passing; I could just make out from the corner of an eye the small black moving patch, while I kept my gaze fixed on the Arab.

It struck me that all I had to do was to turn, walk away, and think no more about it. But the whole beach, pulsing with heat, was pressing on my back. I took some steps towards the stream. The Arab didn't move. After all, there was still some distance between us. Perhaps because of the shadow on his face, he seemed to be grinning at me.

I waited. The heat was beginning to scorch my cheeks, beads of sweat were gathering in my eyebrows. It was just the same sort of heat as at my mother's funeral, and I had the same disagreeable sensations – especially in my forehead, where all the veins seemed to be bursting through the skin. I couldn't stand it any longer, and took another step forward. I knew it was a fool thing to do; I shouldn't get out of the sun by moving on a yard or so. But I took that step, just one step, forward. And then the Arab drew his knife and held it up towards me, athwart the sunlight.

A shaft of light shot upwards from the steel, and I felt as if a long, thin blade transfixed my forehead. At the same moment all the sweat that had accumulated in my eyebrows splashed down on my eyelids, covering them with a warm film of moisture. Beneath a veil of brine and tears my eyes were blinded: I was conscious only of the cymbals of the sun clashing on my skull, and, less distinctly, of the keen blade of light flashing up from the knife, scarring my eyelashes, and gouging into my eyeballs.

Then everything began to reel before my eyes, a fiery gust came from the sea, while the sky cracked in two, from end to end, and a great sheet of flame poured down through the rift. Every nerve in my body was a steel spring, and my grip closed on the revolver. The trigger gave, and the smooth underbelly of the butt jogged my palm. And so, with that crisp, whip-crack sound, it all began. I shook off my sweat and the clinging veil of light. I knew I'd shattered the balance of the day, the spacious calm of this beach on which I had been happy. But I fired four shots more into the inert body, on which they left no visible trace. And each successive shot was another loud, fateful rap on the door of my undoing.

PART TWO

I

I was questioned several times immediately after my arrest. But they were all formal examinations, as to my identity and so forth. At the first of these, which took place at the police station, nobody seemed to take much interest in the case. However, when I was brought before the examining magistrate a week later, I noticed that he eyed me with distinct curiosity. Like the others, he began by asking my name, address and occupation, the date and place of my birth. Then he inquired if I had chosen a lawyer to defend me. I answered 'No,' I hadn't thought about it, and asked him if it was really necessary for me to have one. 'Why do you ask that?' he replied. I replied that I regarded my case as very simple. He smiled. 'Well, it may seem so to you. But we've got to abide by the law, and, if you don't engage a lawyer, the Court will have to appoint one for you.'

It struck me as an excellent arrangement that the authorities should see to details of this kind, and I told him so. He nodded, and agreed that the Code was all that could be desired.

At first I didn't take him quite seriously. The room in which he interviewed me was much like an ordinary sitting-room, with curtained windows and a single lamp standing on the desk. Its light fell on the armchair in which he'd had me sit, while his own face stayed in shadow.

I had read descriptions of such scenes in books, and at first it all seemed like a game. After our conversation, however, I had a good look at him. He was a tall man with clean-cut features, deep-set blue eyes, a big grey moustache and abundant, almost snow-white hair, and he gave me the impression of being highly intelligent and, on the whole, likeable enough. There was only one thing that put one off: his mouth had now and then a rather ugly twist; but it seemed to be only a sort of nervous *tic*. When leaving, I very nearly held out my hand and said 'Good-bye'; just in time I remembered that I'd killed a man.

Next day a lawyer came to my cell; a small, plump, youngish man with sleek black hair. In spite of the heat – I was in my shirt-sleeves – he was wearing a dark suit, stiff collar, and a rather showy tie, with broad black and white stripes. After depositing his brief-case on my bed, he introduced himself, and added that he'd perused the record of my case with the utmost care. His opinion was that it would need cautious handling, but there was every prospect of my getting off, provided I followed his advice. I thanked him, and he said: 'Good. Now let's get down to it.'

Sitting on the bed, he said that they'd been making investigations into my private life. They had learnt that my mother died recently in a Home. Inquiries had been conducted at Marengo and the police informed that I'd shown 'great callousness' at my mother's funeral.

'You must understand,' the lawyer said, 'that I don't relish having to question you about such a matter. But it has much importance and, unless I find some way of answering the charge of "callousness", I shall be handicapped in conducting your defence. And that is where you, and only you, can help me.'

He went on to ask me if I had felt grief on that 'sad occasion'. The question struck me as an odd one; personally I'd have been much embarrassed by having to ask anyone a thing like that.

I answered that in recent years I'd rather lost the habit

of noting my feelings, and hardly knew what to answer. I could truthfully say I'd been quite fond of Mother – but really that didn't mean much. All normal people, I added, as an afterthought, had more or less desired the death of those they loved, at some time or another.

Here the lawyer interrupted me, looking greatly perturbed.

'You must promise me not to say anything of that sort at the trial, or to the examining magistrate.'

I promised, to satisfy him; but I explained that my physical condition at any given moment often influenced my feelings. For instance, on the day I attended Mother's funeral, I was fagged out and only half awake. So really I hardly took stock of what was happening. Anyhow I could assure him of one thing: that I'd rather Mother hadn't died.

The lawyer, however, looked displeased. 'That's not enough,' he said curtly.

After considering for a bit he asked me if he could say that on that day I had kept my feelings under control.

'No,' I said. 'That wouldn't be true.'

He gave me a queer look, as if I slightly revolted him; then informed me, in an almost hostile tone, that in any case the Head of the Home and some of the staff would be cited as witnesses.

'And that might do you a very nasty turn,' he concluded.

When I suggested that Mother's death had no connexion with the charge against me he merely replied that this remark showed I'd never had any dealings with the Law.

Soon after this he left, looking quite vexed. I wished he had stayed longer and I could have explained that I desired his sympathy, not for him to make a better job of my defence but, if I might put it so, spontaneously. I could see that I got on his nerves; he couldn't make me out and, naturally enough, this irritated him. Once or twice I had a mind to assure him that I was just like everybody else; quite an ordinary person. But really that would have served no great purpose, and I let it go – out of laziness as much as anything else.

Later in the day I was taken again to the examining magistrate's office. It was two in the afternoon and, this time, the room was flooded with light – there was only a thin curtain on the window – and extremely hot.

After inviting me to sit down, the magistrate informed me in a very polite tone that, 'owing to unforeseen circumstances', my lawyer was unable to be present. I should be quite entitled, he added, to reserve my answers to his questions until my lawyer could attend.

To this I replied that I could answer for myself. He pressed a bell-push on his desk and a young clerk came in and seated himself just behind me. Then we – I and the magistrate – settled back in our chairs and the examination began. He led off by remarking that I had the reputation of being a taciturn, rather self-centred person, and he'd like to know what I had to say to that. I answered:

'Well, I rarely have anything much to say. So naturally I keep my mouth shut.'

He smiled as on the previous occasion, and agreed that that was the best of reasons. 'In any case,' he added, 'it has little or no importance.'

After a short silence he suddenly leant forward, looked me in the eyes and said, raising his voice a little:

'What really interests me is – you!'

I wasn't quite clear what he meant, so I made no comment.

'There are several things,' he continued, 'that puzzle me, about your crime. I feel sure that you will help me to understand them.'

When I replied that really it was quite simple, he asked

me to give him an account of what I'd done that day. As a matter of fact I had already told him at our first interview – in a summary sort of way, of course – about Raymond, the beach, our swim, the fight, then the beach again, and the five shots I'd fired. But I went over it all again, and after each phrase he nodded. 'Quite so, quite so.' When I described the body lying on the sand, he nodded more emphatically, and said 'Good!' Personally I was tired of repeating the same story; I felt as if I'd never talked so much in all my life before.

After another silence he stood up and said he'd like to help me; I interested him and, with God's help, he would do something for me in my trouble. But, first, he must put a few more questions.

He began by asking bluntly if I'd loved my mother.

'Yes,' I replied, 'like everybody else.' The clerk behind me, who had been typing away at a steady pace, must just then have hit the wrong keys, as I heard him pushing the carriage back and crossing something out.

Next, without any apparent logical connexion, the magistrate sprang another question.

'Why did you fire five consecutive shots?'

I thought for a bit; then explained that they weren't quite consecutive. I fired one at first, and the other four after a short interval.

'Why did you pause between the first and second shot?'

I seemed to see it hovering again before my eyes, the red glow of the beach, and to feel that fiery breath on my cheeks – and, this time, I made no answer.

During the silence which followed, the magistrate kept fidgeting, running his fingers through his hair, half rising, then sitting down again. Finally, planting his elbows on the desk, he bent towards me with a queer expression.

'But why, *why* did you go on firing at a prostrate man?'

Again I found nothing to reply.

The magistrate drew his hand across his forehead and repeated in a slightly different tone:

'I ask you "*Why*?" I insist on your telling me.'

I still kept silent.

Suddenly he rose, walked to a file cabinet standing against the opposite wall, pulled a drawer open, and took from it a silver crucifix, which he was waving as he came back to the desk.

'Do you know who this is?' His voice had changed completely; it was vibrant with emotion.

'Of course I do,' I answered.

That seemed to start him off; he began speaking at a great pace. He told me he believed in God, and that even the worst of sinners could obtain forgiveness of Him. But first he must repent, and become like a little child, with a simple, trustful heart, open to conviction. He was leaning right across the table brandishing his crucifix before my eyes.

As a matter of fact I had great difficulty in following his remarks as, for one thing, the office was so stifling hot and big flies were buzzing round and settling on my cheeks; also because he rather alarmed me. Of course I realized it was absurd to feel like this, considering that, after all, it was I who was the criminal. However, as he continued talking, I did my best to understand, and I gathered that there was only one point in my confession that badly needed clearing up – the fact that I'd waited before firing a second time. All the rest was, so to speak, quite in order; but this completely baffled him.

I started to tell him that he was wrong in insisting on this; the point was of quite minor importance. But, before I could get the words out, he had drawn himself up to his full height, and was asking me very earnestly if I believed in God. When I said 'No', he plumped down into his chair indignantly.

That was unthinkable, he said; all men believe in God, even those who reject Him. Of this he was absolutely sure; if ever he came to doubt it, his life would lose all meaning. 'Do you wish', he asked indignantly, 'my life to have no meaning?' Really I couldn't see how my wishes came into it, and I told him as much.

While I was talking, he thrust the crucifix again just under my nose and shouted: 'I, anyhow, am a Christian. And I pray Him to forgive you for your sins. My poor young man, how can you not believe that He suffered for your sake?'

I noticed that his manner seemed genuinely solicitous when he said, 'My poor young man' – but I was beginning to have enough of it. The room was growing steadily hotter.

As I usually do when I want to get rid of someone whose conversation bores me, I pretended to agree. At which, rather to my surprise, his face lit up.

'You see! You see! Now won't you own that you believe and put your trust in Him?'

I must have shaken my head again, for he sank back in his chair looking limp and dejected.

For some moments there was a silence during which the typewriter, which had been clicking away all the time we talked, caught up with the last remark. Then he gazed at me intently and rather sadly.

'Never in all my experience have I known a soul so case-hardened as yours,' he said in a low tone. 'All the criminals who have come before me until now wept when they saw this symbol of our Lord's sufferings.'

I was on the point of replying that was precisely because

they *were* criminals. But then I realized that I, too, came under that description. Somehow it was an idea to which I never could get reconciled.

To indicate, presumably, that the interview was over, the magistrate stood up. In the same weary tone he asked me a last question: Did I regret what I had done?

After thinking a bit, I said that what I felt was less regret than a kind of vexation – I couldn't find a better word for it. But he didn't seem to understand. This was as far as things went at that day's interview.

I came before the magistrate many times more, but on these occasions my lawyer always accompanied me. The examinations were confined to asking me to amplify my previous statements. Or else the magistrate and my lawyer discussed technicalities. At such times they took very little notice of me and, in any case, the tone of the examinations changed as time went on. The magistrate seemed to have lost interest in me, and to have come to some sort of decision about my case. He never mentioned God again or displayed any of the religious fervour I had found so embarrassing at our first interview. The result was that our relations became more cordial. After a few questions, followed by an exchange of remarks with my lawyer, the magistrate closed the interview. My case was 'taking its course,' as he put it. Sometimes, too, the conversation was of a general order and the magistrate and lawyer encouraged me to join in it. I began to breathe more freely. Neither of the two men, at these times, showed the least hostility towards me, and everything went so smoothly, so amiably, that I had an absurd impression of being 'one of the family'. I can honestly say that during the eleven months these examinations lasted I got so used to them that I was almost surprised at having ever enjoyed anything better than those rare moments when the magistrate, after escorting me to the door of the office, would pat my shoulder and say in a friendly tone: 'Well, Mr Antichrist, that's all for the present!' After which I was made over to my warders.

2

THERE are some things of which I've never cared to talk. And, a few days after I'd been sent to prison, I decided that this phase of my life was one of them. However, as time went by, I came to feel that this aversion had no real substance. In point of fact, during those first few days, I was hardly conscious of being in prison; I had always a vague hope that something would turn up, some agreeable surprise.

The change came soon after Marie's first and only visit. From the day when I got her letter telling me they wouldn't let her come to see me any more, because she wasn't my wife – it was from that day I realized that this cell was my last home, a dead end, as one says.

On the day of my arrest they put me in a biggish room with several other prisoners, mostly Arabs. They grinned when they saw me enter, and asked me what I'd done. I told them I'd killed an Arab, and they kept mum for a while. But presently night began to fall, and one of them explained to me how to lay out my sleeping-mat. By rolling up one end one makes a sort of bolster. All night I felt bugs crawling over my face.

Some days later I was put by myself in a cell, where I slept on a plank bed hinged to the wall. The only other furniture was a latrine bucket and a tin basin. The prison stands on rising ground, and through my little window I had glimpses of the sea. One day when I was hanging on the bars, straining my eyes towards the sunlight playing on the waves, a warder entered and said I had a visitor. I thought it must be Marie, and so it was.

To go to the Visitors' Room, I was taken along a corridor, then up a flight of steps, then along another corridor. It was a very large room, lit by a big bow-window, and divided into three compartments by high iron grilles running transversely. Between the two grilles there was a gap of some thirty feet, a sort of no-man's-land between the prisoners and their friends. I was led to a point exactly opposite Marie, who was wearing her striped dress. On my side of the rails were about a dozen other prisoners, Arabs for the most part. On Marie's side were mostly Moorish women. She was wedged between a small old woman with tight-set lips, and a fat matron, without a hat, who was talking shrilly and gesticulated all the time. Because of the distance between the visitors and prisoners I found I, too, had to raise my voice.

When I came into the room the babel of voices echoing on the bare walls, and the sunlight streaming in, flooding everything in a harsh white glare, made me feel quite dizzy. After the relative darkness and the silence of my cell it took me some moments to get used to these conditions. After a bit, however, I came to see each face quite clearly, lit up as if a spotlight played on it.

I noticed a prison official seated at each end of the no-man's-land between the grilles. The native prisoners and their relations on the other side were squatting opposite each other. They didn't raise their voices and, in spite of the din, managed to converse almost in whispers. This murmur of voices coming from below made a sort of accompaniment to the conversations going on above their heads. I took stock of all this very quickly, and moved a step forward towards Marie. She was pressing her brown, sun-tanned face to the

76

bars and smiling as hard as she could. I thought she was looking very pretty, but somehow couldn't bring myself to tell her so.

'Well?' she asked, pitching her voice very high. 'What about it? Are you all right, have you everything you want?'

'Oh, yes. I've everything I want.'

We were silent for some moments; Marie went on smiling. The fat woman was bawling at the prisoner beside me, her husband presumably, a tall, fair, pleasant-looking-man.

'Jeanne refused to have him,' she yelled. – 'That's just too bad,' the man replied. – 'Yes, and I told her you'd take him back the moment you get out; but she wouldn't hear of it.'

Marie shouted across the gap that Raymond sent me his best wishes, and I said, 'Thanks.' But my voice was drowned by my neighbour's asking, 'if he was quite fit'. The fat woman gave a laugh. 'Fit? I should say he is! The picture of health.'

Meanwhile the prisoner on my left, a youngster with thin, girlish hands, never said a word. His eyes, I noticed, were fixed on the little old woman opposite him, and she returned his gaze with a sort of hungry passion. But I had to stop looking at them as Marie was shouting to me that we mustn't lose hope.

'Certainly not,' I answered. My gaze fell on her shoulders and I had a sudden longing to squeeze them, through the thin dress. Its silky texture fascinated me, and I had a feeling that the hope she spoke of centred on it somehow. I imagine something of the same sort was in Marie's mind, for she went on smiling, looking straight at me.

'It'll all come right, you'll see, and then we shall get married.'

All I could see of her now was the white flash of her teeth, and the little puckers round her eyes. I answered: 'Do you really think so?' but chiefly because I felt it up to me to answer something.

She started talking very fast in the same high-pitched voice.

'Yes, you'll be acquitted, and we'll go bathing again, Sundays.'

The woman beside Marie was still yelling away, telling her husband that she'd left a basket for him in the prison office. She gave a list of the things she'd brought and told him to mind and check them carefully, as some had cost quite a lot. The youngster on my other side and his mother were still gazing mournfully at each other, and the murmur of the Arabs droned on below us. The light outside seemed to be surging up against the window, seeping through, and smearing the faces of the people facing it with a coat of yellow oil.

I began to feel slightly squeamish, and wished I could leave. The strident voice beside me was jarring on my ears. But, on the other hand, I wanted to have the most I could of Marie's company. I've no idea how much time passed. I remember Marie's describing to me her work, with that set smile always on her face. There wasn't a moment's let-up in the noise – shouts, conversations, and always that muttering undertone. The only oasis of silence was made by the young fellow and the old dame gazing into each other's eyes.

Then, one by one, the Arabs were led away; almost everyone fell silent when the first one left. The little old woman pressed herself against the bars and at the same moment a warder tapped her son's shoulder. He called '*Au revoir*, Mother,' and, slipping her hand between the bars, she gave him a small, slow wave with it.

No sooner was she gone than a man, hat in hand, took her place. A prisoner was led up to the empty place beside me, and the two started a brisk exchange of remarks – not loud, however, as the room had become relatively quiet. Someone came and called away the man on my right and his wife shouted at him – she didn't seem to realize it was no longer necessary to shout – 'Now, mind you look after yourself, dear, and don't do anything rash!'

My turn came next. Marie threw me a kiss. I looked back as I walked away. She hadn't moved; her face was still pressed to the rails, her lips still parted in that tense, twisted smile.

Soon after this I had a letter from her. And it was then that the things I've never liked to talk about began. Not that they were particularly terrible; I've no wish to exaggerate and I suffered less than others. Still, there was one thing in those early days that was really irksome: my habit of thinking like a free man. For instance, I would suddenly be seized with a desire to go down to the beach for a swim. And merely to have imagined the sound of ripples at my feet, and then the smooth feel of the water on my body as I struck out, and the wonderful sensation of relief it gave, brought home still more cruelly the narrowness of my cell.

Still, that phase lasted a few months only. Afterwards, I had prisoner's thoughts. I waited for the daily walk in the courtyard, or a visit from my lawyer. As for the rest of the time, I managed quite well, really. I've often thought that had I been compelled to live in the trunk of a dead tree, with nothing to do but gaze up at the patch of sky just overhead, I'd have got used to it by degrees. I'd have learnt to watch for the passing of birds or drifting clouds, as I had come to watch for my lawyer's odd neckties, or, in another world, to wait patiently till Sunday for a spell of love-making with Marie. Well, here anyhow, I wasn't penned in a hollow tree-trunk. There were others in the world worse off than I was. I remembered it had been one of

Mothers' pet ideas – she was always voicing it – that in the long run one gets used to anything.

Usually, however, I didn't think things out so far. Those first months were trying, of course; but the very effort I had to make helped me through them. For instance, I was plagued by the desire for a woman – which was natural enough, considering my age. I never thought of Marie especially. I was obsessed by thoughts of this woman or that, of all the ones I'd had, all the circumstances under which I'd loved them; so much so that the cell grew crowded with their faces, ghosts of my old passions. That unsettled me, no doubt; but, at least, it served to kill time.

I gradually became quite friendly with the chief gaoler, who went the rounds with the kitchen-hands at meal-times. It was he who brought up the subject of women. 'That's what the men here grumble about most,' he told me. I said I felt like that myself. 'There's something unfair about it,' I added, 'like hitting a man when he's down.' – 'But that's the whole point of it,' he said; 'that's why you fellows are kept in prison.' – 'I don't follow.' – 'Liberty,' he said, 'means that. You're being deprived of your liberty.' It had never before struck me in that light, but I saw his point. 'That's true,' I said. 'Otherwise it wouldn't be a punishment.' The gaoler nodded. 'Yes, you're different, you can use your brains. The others can't. Still, those fellows find a way out; they do it by themselves.' With which remark the gaoler left my cell. Next day I did like the others.

The lack of cigarettes, too, was a trial. When I was brought to the prison, they took away my belt, my shoe-laces, and the contents of my pockets, including my cigarettes. Once I had been given a cell to myself I asked to be given back anyhow the cigarettes. Smoking was forbidden, they informed me. That, perhaps, was what got me down the most; in fact, I suffered really badly during the first few days. I even tore off splinters from my plank bed and sucked them. All day long I felt faint and bilious. It passed my understanding why I shouldn't be allowed even to smoke; it could have done no one any harm. Later on, I understood the idea behind it; this privation, too, was part of my punishment. But, by the time I understood, I'd lost the craving, so it had ceased to be a punishment.

Except for these privations, I wasn't too unhappy. Yet again, the whole problem was: how to kill time. After a while, however, once I'd learnt the trick of remembering things, I never had a moment's boredom. Sometimes I would exercise my memory on my bedroom, and, starting from a corner, make the round, noting every object I saw on the way. At first it was over in a minute or two. But each time I repeated the experience, it took a little longer. I made a point of visualizing every piece of furniture, and each article upon or in it, and then every detail of each article, and finally the details of the details, so to speak: a tiny dent or incrustation, or a chipped edge, and the exact grain and colour of the woodwork. At the same time I forced myself to keep my inventory in mind from start to finish, in the right order and omitting no item. With the result that, after a few weeks, I could spend hours merely in listing the objects in my bedroom. I found that the more I thought, the more details, half-forgotten or malobserved, floated up from my memory. There seemed no end to them.

So I learned that even after a single day's experience of the outside world a man could easily live a hundred years in prison. He'd have laid up enough memories never to be bored. Obviously, in one way, this was a compensation.

Then there was sleep. To begin with, I slept badly at night and never in the day. But gradually my nights became better and I managed to doze off in the daytime as well. In fact, during the last months, I must have slept sixteen or eighteen hours out of the twenty-four. So there remained only six hours to fill – with meals, relieving nature, my memories . . . and the story of the Czech.

One day, when inspecting my straw mattress, I found a bit of newspaper stuck to its underside. The paper was yellow with age, almost transparent, but one could still make out the letter-print. It was the story of a crime. The first part was missing, but one gathered that its scene was some village in Czechoslovakia. One of the villagers had left his home to try his luck abroad. After twenty-five years, having made a fortune, he returned to his country with his wife and child. Meanwhile his mother and sister had been running a small hotel in the village where he was born. He decided to give them a surprise and, leaving his wife and child in another inn, he went to stay at his mother's place, booking a room under an assumed name. His mother and sister completely failed to recognize him. At dinner that evening he showed them a large sum of money he had on him, and in the course of the night they slaughtered him with a hammer. After taking the money they flung the body into the river. Next morning his wife came and, without thinking, betrayed the guest's identity. His mother hanged herself. His sister threw herself into a well. I must have read that story thousands of times. In one way it sounded most unlikely; in another, it was plausible enough. Anyhow, to my mind, the man was asking for trouble; one shouldn't play fool tricks of that sort.

So, what with long bouts of sleep, my memories, readings of that scrap of newspaper, the tides of light and darkness, the days slipped by. I'd read, of course, that in gaol one ends up by losing track of time. But this had never meant anything definite to me. I hadn't grasped how days could be at once long and short. Long, no doubt, as periods to live through, but so distended that they ended up by overlapping on each other. In fact I never thought of days as such; only the words 'yesterday' and 'tomorrow' still kept some meaning.

When, one morning the warder informed me I'd now been six months in gaol, I believed him – but the words conveyed nothing to my mind. To me it seemed like one and the same day that had been going on since I'd been in my cell, and that I'd been doing the same thing all the time.

After the gaoler left me I shined up my tin pannikin and studied my face in it. My expression was terribly serious, I thought, even when I tried to smile. I held the pannikin at different angles, but always my face had the same mournful, tense expression.

The sun was setting and it was the hour of which I'd rather not speak – 'the nameless hour', I called it – when evening sounds were creeping up from all the floors of the prison in a sort of stealthy procession. I went to the barred window and in the last rays looked once again at my re-flected face. It was as serious as before; and that wasn't surprising, as just then I was feeling serious. But, at the same time, I heard something that I hadn't heard for months. It was the sound of a voice; my own voice, there was no mistaking it. And I recognized it as the voice that for many a day of late had been buzzing in my ears. So I knew that all this time I'd been talking to myself.

And something I'd been told came back to me; a remark made by the nurse at Mother's funeral. No, there was no way out, and no one can imagine what the evenings are like in prison.

3

On the whole I can't say that those months passed slowly; another summer was on its way almost before I realized the first was over. And I knew that with the first really hot days something new was in store for me. My case was down for the last Sessions of the Assize Court, and that Sessions was due to end some time in June.

The day on which my trial started was one of brilliant sunshine. My lawyer assured me the case would take only two or three days. 'From what I hear,' he added, 'the Court will despatch your case as quickly as possible, as it isn't the most important one on the Cause List. There's a case of parricide immediately after, which will take them some time.'

They came for me at half past seven in the morning and I was conveyed to the Law Courts in the prison van. The two policemen led me into a small room that smelt of darkness. We sat near a door through which came sounds of voices, shouts, chairs scraping on the floor; a vague hubbub which reminded me of one of those small town 'socials' when, after the concert's over, the hall is cleared for dancing.

One of my policemen told me the judges hadn't arrived yet, and offered me a cigarette, which I declined. After a bit he asked me if I was feeling nervous. I said 'No', and that the prospect of witnessing a trial rather interested me; I'd never had occasion to attend one before.

'Maybe,' the other policeman said. 'But after an hour or two one's had enough of it.'

After a while a small electric bell purred in the room. They unfastened my handcuffs, opened the door, and led me to the prisoner's dock.

There was a great crowd in the courtroom. Though the venetian blinds were down, light was filtering through the chinks, and the air was stifling hot already. The windows had been kept shut. I sat down, and the police officers took their stand on each side of my chair.

It was then that I noticed a row of faces opposite me. These people were staring hard at me, and I guessed they were the jury. But somehow I didn't see them as individuals. I felt as one does just after boarding a tram and one's conscious of all the people on the opposite seat staring at one in the hope of finding something in one's appearance to amuse them. Of course I knew this was an absurd comparison; what these people were looking for in me wasn't anything to laugh at, but signs of criminality. Still, the difference wasn't so very great, and, anyhow, that's the idea I got.

What with the crowd and the stuffiness of the air I was feeling a bit dizzy. I ran my eyes round the courtroom but couldn't recognize any of the faces. At first I could hardly believe that all these people had come on my account. It was such a new experience, being a focus of interest; in the ordinary way no one ever paid much attention to me. 'What a crush!' I remarked to the policeman on my left, and he explained that the newspapers were responsible for it. He pointed to a group of men at a table just below the jury-box. 'There they are!' – 'Who?' I asked, and he replied, 'The Press.' One of them, he added, was an old friend of his.

A moment later the man he'd mentioned looked our way and, coming to the dock, shook hands warmly with the policeman. The journalist was an elderly man with a rather grim expression, but his manner was quite pleasant. Just then, I noticed that almost all the people in the courtroom were greeting each other, exchanging remarks and forming groups – behaving, in fact, as in a club where the company of others of one's own tastes and standing makes one feel at ease. That, no doubt, explained the odd impression I had of being *de trop* here, a sort of gate-crasher.

However, the journalist addressed me quite amiably, and said he hoped all would go well for me. I thanked him, and he added with a smile:

'You know, we've been featuring you a bit. We're always rather short of copy in the summer, and there's been precious little to write about except your case and the one that's coming on after it. I expect you've heard about it; it's a case of parricide.'

He drew my attention to one of the group at the Press table, a plump, small man with huge black-rimmed glasses, who made one think of an over-fed weasel.

'That chap's the special correspondent of one of the Paris dailies. As a matter of fact he didn't come on your account. He was sent for the parricide case, but they've asked him to cover yours as well.'

It was on the tip of my tongue to say, 'That was very kind of them,' but then I thought it would sound silly. With a friendly wave of his hand he left us, and for some minutes nothing happened.

Then, accompanied by some colleagues, my lawyer bustled in, in his gown. He went up to the Press table and shook hands with the journalists. They remained laughing and chatting together, all seemingly very much at home here, until a bell rang shrilly and everyone went to his place. My lawyer came up to me, shook hands, and advised me to answer all the questions as briefly as possible, not to volunteer information, and to rely on him to see me through.

I heard a chair scrape on my left, and a tall, thin man wearing pince-nez settled the folds of his red gown as he

86

took his seat. The public prosecutor, I gathered. A clerk of the court announced that Their Honours were entering and at the same moment two big electric fans started buzzing overhead. Three judges, two in black and the third in scarlet, with brief-cases under their arms, entered and walked briskly to the bench, which was several feet above the level of the courtroom floor. The man in scarlet took the central, high-backed chair, placed his cap of office on the table, ran a handkerchief over his small bald crown, and announced that the hearing would now begin.

The journalists had their fountain-pens ready; they all wore the same expression of slightly ironical indifference, with the exception of one, a much younger man than his colleagues, in grey flannels with a blue tie, who, leaving his pen on the table, was gazing hard at me. He had a plain, rather chunky face; what held my attention was his eyes, very pale, clear eyes, riveted on me, though not betraying any definite emotion. For a moment I had an odd impression, as if I were being scrutinized by myself. That – and the fact that I was unfamiliar with court procedure – may explain why I didn't follow very well the opening phases: the drawing of lots for the jury, the various questions put by the presiding judge to the prosecutor, the foreman of the jury and my counsel (each time he spoke all the jurymen's heads swung round together towards the bench), the hurried reading of the charge-sheet, in the course of which I recognized some familiar names of people and places, then some supplementary questions put to my lawyer.

Next, the judge announced that the court would call over the witness-list. Some of the names read out by the clerk rather surprised me. From amongst the crowd, which until now I had seen as a mere blur of faces, rose, one after the other, Raymond, Masson, Salamano, the door-keeper from the Home, old Pérez, and Marie, who gave me a little

87

nervous wave of her hand before following the others out by a side door. I was thinking how strange it was I hadn't noticed any of them before when I heard the last name called, that of Céleste. As he rose, I noticed beside him the quaint little woman with a mannish coat and brisk, decided air, who had shared my table at the restaurant. She had her eyes fixed on me, I noticed. But I hadn't time to wonder about her; the judge had started speaking again.

He said that the trial proper was about to begin, and he need hardly say that he expected the public to refrain from any demonstration whatsoever. He explained that he was there to supervise the proceedings, as a sort of umpire, and he would take a scrupulously impartial view of the case. The verdict of the jury would be interpreted by him in a spirit of justice. Finally, at the least sign of a disturbance he would have the court cleared.

The day was stoking up. Some of the public were fanning themselves with newspapers, and there was a constant rustle of crumpled paper. On a sign from the presiding judge the clerk of the court brought three fans of plaited straw, which the three judges promptly put in action.

My examination began at once. The judge questioned me quite calmly and even, I thought, with a hint of cordiality. For the nth time I was asked to give particulars of my identity and, though heartily sick of this formality, I realized that it was natural enough; after all, it would be a shocking thing for the court to be trying the wrong man.

The judge then launched into an account of what I'd done, stopping every two or three sentences to ask me, 'Is that correct?' To which I always replied, 'Yes, sir,' as my lawyer had advised me. It was a long business, as the judge lingered on each detail. Meanwhile the journalists scribbled busily away. But I was sometimes conscious of the eyes of the youngest fixed on me; also those of the queer little robot woman. The jurymen, however, were all gazing at the red-robed judge, and I was again reminded of the row of passengers on one side of a tram. Presently he gave a slight cough, turned some pages of his file, and, still fanning his face, addressed me gravely.

He now proposed, he said, to touch on certain matters which, on a superficial view, might seem foreign to the case, but actually were highly relevant. I guessed that he was going to talk about Mother, and at the same moment realized how odious I would find this. His first question was: Why had I sent my mother to an Institution? I replied that the reason was simple; I hadn't enough money to see that she was properly looked after at home. Then he asked if the parting hadn't caused me distress. I explained that neither Mother nor I expected much of one another – or, for that matter, of anybody else; so both of us had got used to the new conditions easily enough. The judge then said that he had no wish to press the point, and asked the Prosecutor if he could think of any more questions that should be put to me at this stage.

The prosecutor, who had his back half turned to me, said, without looking in my direction, that, subject to His Honour's approval, he would like to know if I'd gone back to the stream with the intention of killing the Arab. I said 'No.' In that case, why had I taken a revolver with me, and why go back precisely to that spot? I said it was a matter of pure chance. The Prosecutor then observed in a nasty tone: 'Very good. That will be all for the present.'

I couldn't quite follow what came next. Anyhow, after some palavering between the Bench, the prosecutor and my counsel, the presiding judge announced that the court would now rise; there was an adjournment till the afternoon, when evidence would be taken.

Almost before I knew what was happening, I was rushed

out to the prison van, which drove me back, and I was given my midday meal. After a short time, just enough for me to realize how tired I was feeling, they came for me. I was back in the same room, confronting the same faces, and the whole thing started again. But the heat had meanwhile much increased, and by some miracle fans had been procured for everyone; the jury, my lawyer, the prosecutor, and some of the pressmen, too. The young man and the robot woman were still at their places. But they were not fanning themselves and, as before, they never took their eyes off me.

I wiped the sweat from my face, but I was barely conscious of where or who I was until I heard the Warden of the Home called to the witness-box. When asked if my mother had complained about my conduct, he said 'Yes', but that didn't mean much; almost all the inmates of the Home had grievances against their relatives. The judge asked him to be more explicit; did she reproach me with having sent her to the Home, and he said 'Yes' again. But this time he didn't qualify his answer.

To another question he replied that on the day of the funeral he was somewhat surprised by my calmness. Asked to explain what he meant by 'my calmness', the Warden lowered his eyes and stared at his shoes for a moment. Then he explained that I hadn't wanted to see Mother's body, or shed a single tear, and that I'd left immediately the funeral ended, without lingering at her grave. Another thing had surprised him. One of the undertaker's men told him that I didn't know my mother's age. There was a short silence; then the judge asked him if he might take it that he was referring to the prisoner in the dock. The Warden seemed puzzled by this, and the judge explained: 'It's a formal question. I am bound to put it.'

The prosecutor was then asked if he had any questions

to put, and he answered loudly: 'Certainly not! I have all I want.' His tone and the look of triumph on his face, as he glanced at me, were so marked that I felt as I hadn't felt for ages. I had a foolish desire to burst into tears. For the first time I'd realized how all these people loathed me.

After asking the jury and my lawyer if they had any questions, the judge heard the door-keeper's evidence. On stepping into the box the man threw a glance at me, then looked away. Replying to questions, he said that I'd declined to see Mother's body, I'd smoked cigarettes and slept, and drunk *café au lait*. It was then I felt a sort of wave of indignation spreading through the courtroom, and for the first time I understood that I was guilty. They got the door-keeper to repeat what he had said about the coffee and my smoking. The prosecutor turned to me again, with a gloating look in his eyes. My counsel asked the door-keeper if he, too, hadn't smoked. But the prosecutor took strong exception to this. 'I'd like to know', he cried indignantly, 'who is on trial in this court. Or does my friend think that by aspersing a witness for the prosecution he will shake the evidence, the abundant and cogent evidence, against his client?' None the less, the judge told the door-keeper to answer the question.

The old fellow fidgeted a bit. Then, 'Well, I know I didn't ought to have done it,' he mumbled, 'but I did take a fag from the young gentleman when he offered it – just out of politeness.'

The judge asked me if I had any comment to make. 'None,' I said, 'except that the witness is quite right. It's true I offered him a cigarette.'

The door-keeper looked at me with surprise and a sort of gratitude. Then, after humming and hawing for a bit, he volunteered the statement that it was he who'd suggested I should have some coffee.

My lawyer was exultant. 'The jury will appreciate', he said, 'the importance of this admission.'

The prosecutor, however, was promptly on his feet again. 'Quite so,' he boomed above our heads. 'The jury will appreciate it. And they will draw the conclusion that, though a third party might inadvertently offer him a cup of coffee, the prisoner, in common decency, should have refused it, if only out of respect for the dead body of the poor woman who had brought him into the world.'

After which the door-keeper went back to his seat.

When Thomas Pérez was called, a court officer had to help him to the box. Pérez stated that, though he had been a great friend of my mother, he had met me once only, on the day of the funeral. Asked how I had behaved that day, he said:

'Well, I was most upset, you know. Far too much upset to notice things. My grief sort of blinded me, I think. It had been a great shock, my dear friend's death; in fact I fainted during the funeral. So I didn't hardly notice the young gentleman at all.'

The prosecutor asked him to tell the court if he'd seen me weep. And when Pérez answered 'No,' added emphatically: 'I trust the jury will take note of this reply.'

My lawyer rose at once, and asked Pérez in a tone that seemed to me needlessly aggressive:

'Now think well, my man! Can you swear you saw he didn't shed a tear?'

Pérez answered, 'No.'

At this some people tittered and my lawyer, pushing back one sleeve of his gown, said sternly:

'That is typical of the way this case is being conducted. No attempt is being made to elicit the true facts.'

The prosecutor ignored this remark; he was making

dabs with his pencil on the cover of his brief, seemingly quite indifferent.

There was a break of five minutes, during which my lawyer told me the case was going very well indeed. Then Céleste was called. He was announced as a witness for the defence. The defence meant me.

Now and again Céleste threw me a glance; he kept squeezing his panama hat between his hands as he gave evidence. He was in his best suit, the one he wore when sometimes of a Sunday he went with me to the races. But evidently he hadn't been able to get his collar on; the top of his shirt, I noticed, was secured only by a brass stud. Asked if I was one of his customers, he said, 'Yes, and a friend as well.' Asked to state his opinion of me, he said that I was 'all right' and, when told to explain what he meant by that, he replied that everyone knew what that meant. 'Was I a secretive sort of man?' – 'No,' he answered, 'I shouldn't call him that. But he isn't one to waste his breath, like a lot of folks.'

The prosecutor asked him if I always settled my monthly bill at his restaurant when he presented it. Céleste laughed. 'Oh, he paid on the nail all right. But the bills were just details, like, between him and me.' Then he was asked to say what he thought about the crime. He placed his hands on the rail of the box and one could see he had a speech all ready.

'To my mind it was just an accident, or a stroke of bad luck, if you prefer. And a thing like that takes you off your guard.'

He wanted to continue, but the judge cut him short. 'Quite so. That's all, thank you.'

For a bit Céleste seemed flabbergasted; then he explained that he hadn't finished what he wanted to say. They told him to continue, but to make it brief.

He only repeated that it was 'just an accident.'

'That's as it may be,' the judge observed. 'But what we are here for is to try such accidents, according to law. You can stand down.'

Céleste turned and gazed at me. His eyes were moist and his lips trembling It was exactly as if he'd said: 'Well, I've done my best for you, old chap. I'm afraid it hasn't helped much. I'm sorry.'

I didn't say anything, or make any movement, but for the first time in my life I wanted to kiss a man.

The judge repeated his order to stand down and Céleste returned to his place amongst the crowd. During the rest of the hearing he remained there, leaning forward, elbows on knees and his panama between his hands, not missing a word of the proceedings.

It was Marie's turn next. She had a hat on, and still looked quite pretty, though I much preferred her with her hair free. From where I was I had glimpses of the soft curves of her breasts, and her underlip had the little pout that always fascinated me. She appeared very nervous.

The first question was: How long had she known me? Since the time when she was in our office, she replied. Then the judge asked her what were the relations between us, and she said she was my girl friend. Answering another question, she admitted promising to marry me. The prosecutor, who had been studying a document in front of him, asked her rather sharply when our 'liaison' had begun. She gave the date. He then observed with a would-be casual air that apparently she meant the day following my mother's funeral. After letting this sink in he remarked in a slightly ironic tone that obviously this was a 'delicate topic' and he could enter into the young lady's feelings, but – and here his voice grew sterner – his duty obliged him to waive considerations of delicacy.

After making this announcement he asked Marie to give a full account of our doings on the day when I had 'intercourse' with her for the first time. Marie wouldn't answer at first, but the prosecutor insisted, and then she told him that we had met at the baths, gone together to the pictures, and then to my place. He then informed the court that, as a result of certain statements made by Marie at the proceedings before the magistrate, he had studied the cinema programmes of that date, and turning to Marie asked her to name the film that we had gone to see. In a very low voice she said it was a picture with Fernandel in it. By the time she had finished, the courtroom was so still you could have heard a pin drop.

Looking very grave, the prosecutor drew himself up to his full height and, pointing at me, said in such a tone that I could have sworn he was genuinely moved:

'Gentlemen of the jury, I would have you note that on the next day after his mother's funeral that man was visiting the swimming-pool, starting a liaison with a girl, and going to see a comic film. That is all I wish to say.'

When he sat down there was the same dead silence. Then all of a sudden Marie burst into tears. He'd got it all wrong, she said; it wasn't a bit like that really, he'd bullied her into saying the opposite of what she meant. She knew me very well, and she was sure I hadn't done anything really wrong – and so on. At a sign from the presiding judge, one of the court officers led her away, and the hearing continued.

Hardly anyone seemed to listen to Masson, the next witness. He stated that I was a respectable young fellow; 'and what's more, a very decent chap.' Nor did they pay any more attention to Salamano, when he told them how kind I'd always been to his dog, or when, in answer to a question about my mother and myself, he said that really Mother and I had very little in common and that explained why I'd fixed up for her to enter the Home. 'You've got to under-stand', he added. 'You've got to understand.' But no one seemed to understand. He was told to stand down.

Raymond was the next, and last, witness. He gave me a little wave of his hand and led off by saying I was innocent. The judge rebuked him.

'You are here to give evidence, not your views on the case, and you must confine yourself to answering the questions put you.'

He was then asked to make clear his relations with the deceased, and Raymond took this opportunity of ex-plaining that it was he, not I, against whom the dead man had a grudge, because he, Raymond, had beaten up his sister. The judge asked him if the deceased had no reason to dislike me, too. Raymond told him that my presence on the beach that morning was a pure coincidence.

'How comes it then,' the prosecutor inquired, 'that the letter which led up to this tragedy was the prisoner's work?'

Raymond replied that this, too, was due to mere chance.

To which the prosecutor retorted that in this case 'chance' or 'mere coincidence' seemed to play a remarkably large part. Was it by chance that I hadn't intervened when Ray-mond assaulted his mistress? Did this convenient term 'chance' account for my having vouched for Raymond at the police station and having made, on that occasion, state-ments extravagantly favourable to him? In conclusion, he asked Raymond to state what were his means of liveli-hood.

On his describing himself as a warehouseman, the prose-cutor informed the jury it was common knowledge that the witness lived on the immoral earnings of women. I, he said, was this man's intimate friend and associate; in fact, the whole background of the crime was of the most squalid description. And what made it even more odious was the personality of the prisoner, an inhuman monster wholly without moral sense.

Raymond began to expostulate, and my lawyer, too, protested. They were told that the prosecutor must be allowed to finish his remarks.

'I have nearly done,' he said; then turned to Raymond. 'Was the prisoner your friend?'

'Certainly. We were the best of pals, as they say.'

The prosecutor then put me the same question. I looked hard at Raymond, and he did not turn away.

Then, 'Yes', I answered.

The prosecutor turned towards the jury.

'Not only did the man before you in the dock indulge in the most shameful orgies on the day following his mother's funeral. He killed a man cold-bloodedly, in pursuance of some sordid vendetta in the underworld of prostitutes and pimps. That, gentlemen of the jury, is the type of man the prisoner is.'

No sooner had he sat down than my lawyer, out of all patience, raised his arms so high that his sleeves fell back, showing the full length of his starched shirtcuffs.

'Is my client on trial for having buried his mother, or for killing a man?' he asked.

There were some titters in court. But then the prosecutor sprang to his feet, and, draping his gown round him, said he was amazed at his friend's ingenuousness in failing to see that between these two elements of the case there was a vital link. They hung together psychologically, if he might put it so. 'In short,' he concluded, speaking with great vehemence, 'I accuse the prisoner of behaving at his mother's funeral in a way that showed he was already a criminal at heart.'

These words seemed to make much effect on the jury and public. My lawyer merely shrugged his shoulders and wiped the sweat from his forehead. But obviously he was rattled, and I had a feeling things weren't going well for me.

Soon after this incident the court rose. As I was being taken from the courthouse to the prison van, I was conscious for a few brief moments of the once familiar feel of a summer evening out of doors. And, sitting in the darkness of my moving cell, I recognized, echoing in my tired brain, all the characteristic sounds of a town I'd loved, and of a certain hour of the day which I had always particularly enjoyed. The shouts of newspaper-boys in the already languid air, the last calls of birds in the public garden, the cries of sandwich-vendors, the screech of trams at the steep corners of the upper town, and that faint rustling overhead as darkness sifted down upon the harbour – all these sounds made my return to prison like a blind man's journey along a route whose every inch he knows by heart.

Yes, this was the evening hour when – how long ago it seemed! – I always felt so well content with life. Then, what awaited me was a night of easy, dreamless sleep. This was the same hour, but with a difference; I was returning to a cell and what awaited me was a night haunted by forebodings of the coming day. And so I learnt that familiar paths traced in the dusk of summer evenings may lead as well to prison as to innocent, carefree sleep.

4

IT is always interesting, even in the prisoner's dock, to hear oneself being talked about. And certainly in the speeches of my lawyer and the prosecuting counsel a great deal was said about me; more, in fact, about me personally than about my crime.

Really there wasn't any very great difference between the two speeches. Counsel for the defence raised his arms to heaven and pleaded Guilty, but with extenuating circumstances. The prosecutor made similar gestures; he agreed that I was guilty, but denied extenuating circumstances.

One thing about this phase of the trial was rather irksome. Quite often, interested as I was in what they had to say, I was tempted to put in a word, myself. But my lawyer had advised me not to. 'You won't do your case any good by talking,' he had warned me. In fact there seemed to be a conspiracy to exclude me from the proceedings; I wasn't to have any say and my fate was to be decided out of hand.

It was quite an effort at times for me to refrain from cutting them all short, and saying: 'But, damn it all, who's on trial in this court, I'd like to know? It's a serious matter for a man, being accused of murder. And I've something really important to tell you.'

However, on second thoughts, I found I had nothing to say. In any case, I must admit that hearing oneself talked about loses its interest very soon. The prosecutor's speech, especially, began to bore me before he was half-way through it. The only things that really caught my attention were occasional phrases, his gestures, and some elaborate tirades – but these were isolated patches.

What he was aiming at, I gathered, was to show that my crime was premeditated. I remember his saying at one moment, 'I can prove this, gentlemen of the jury, to the hilt. First, you have the facts of the crime, which are as clear as daylight. And then you have what I may call the night side of this case, the dark workings of a criminal mentality.'

He began by summing up the facts, from my mother's

death onwards. He stressed my heartlessness, my inability to state Mother's age, my visit to the bathing-pool where I met Marie, our matinée at the pictures where a Fernandel film was showing, and finally my return with Marie to my rooms. I didn't quite follow his remarks at first as he kept on mentioning 'the prisoner's mistress', whereas for me she was just 'Marie'. Then he came to the subject of Raymond. It seemed to me that his way of treating the facts showed a certain shrewdness. All he said sounded quite plausible. I'd written the letter in collusion with Raymond so as to entice his mistress to his room and subject her to ill-treatment by a man 'of more than dubious reputation'. Then, on the beach, I'd provoked a brawl with Raymond's enemies, in the course of which Raymond was wounded. I'd asked him for his revolver and gone back myself with the intention of using it. Then I'd shot the Arab. After the first shot I waited. Then, 'to be certain of making a good job of it', I fired four more shots deliberately, point blank and in cold blood, at my victim.

'That is my case,' he said. 'I have described to you the series of events which led this man to kill the deceased, fully aware of what he was doing. I emphasize this point. We are not concerned with an act of homicide committed on a sudden impulse which might serve as extenuation. I ask you to note, gentlemen of the jury, that the prisoner is an educated man. You will have observed the way in which he answered my questions; he is intelligent and he knows the value of words. And I repeat that it is quite impossible to assume that, when he committed the crime, he was unaware what he was doing.'

I noticed that he laid stress on my 'intelligence'. It puzzled me rather why what would count as a good point in an ordinary person should be used against an accused man as an overwhelming proof of his guilt. While thinking this over, I missed what he said next, until I heard him exclaim indignantly: 'And has he uttered a word of regret for his most odious crime? Not one word, gentlemen. Not once in the course of these proceedings did this man show the least contrition.'

Turning towards the dock, he pointed a finger at me, and went on in the same strain. I really couldn't understand why he harped on this point so much. Of course I had to own that he was right; I didn't feel much regret for what I'd done. Still, to my mind he overdid it, and I'd have liked to have a chance of explaining to him, in a quite friendly, almost affectionate way, that I have never been able really to regret anything in all my life. I've always been far too much absorbed in the present moment, or the immediate future, to think back. Of course, in the position into which I had been forced, there was no question of my speaking to anyone in that tone. I hadn't the right to show any friendly feeling or possess good intentions. And I tried to follow what came next, as the prosecutor was now considering what he called my 'soul'.

He said he'd studied it closely – and had found a blank, 'literally nothing, gentlemen of the jury'. Really, he said, I had no soul, there was nothing human about me, not one of those moral qualities which normal men possess had any place in my mentality. 'No doubt', he added, 'we should not reproach him with this. We cannot blame a man for lacking what it was never in his power to acquire. But in a criminal court the wholly passive ideal of tolerance must give place to a sterner, loftier ideal, that of Justice. Especially when this lack of every decent instinct is such as that of the man before you, a menace to society.' He proceeded to discuss my conduct towards my mother, repeating what he had said in the course of the hearing. But he spoke at much greater length of my crime; at such length, indeed, that I lost the thread and was conscious only of the steadily increasing heat.

A moment came when the prosecutor paused and, after a short silence, said in a low, vibrant voice: 'This same court, gentlemen, will be called on to try tomorrow that most odious of crimes, the murder of a father by his son.' To his mind, such a crime was almost unimaginable. But, he ventured to hope, Justice would be meted out without faltering. And yet, he made bold to say, the horror that even the crime of parricide inspired in him paled beside the loathing inspired by my callousness.

'This man, who is morally guilty of his mother's death, is no less unfit to have a place in the community than that other man who did to death the father who begat him. And, indeed, the one crime led on to the other; the first of these two criminals, the man in the dock, set a precedent, if I may put it so, and authorized the second crime. Yes, gentlemen, I am convinced' – here he raised his voice a tone – 'that you will not find I am exaggerating the case against the prisoner when I say that he is also guilty of the murder to be tried tomorrow in this court. And I look to you for a verdict accordingly.'

The prosecutor paused again, to wipe the sweat off his face. He then explained that his duty was a painful one, but he would do it without flinching. 'This man has, I repeat, no place in a community whose basic principles he flouts without compunction. Nor, heartless as he is, has he any claim to mercy. I ask you to impose the extreme penalty of the law; and I ask it without a qualm. In the course of a long career, in which it has often been my duty to ask for a capital sentence, never have I felt that painful duty weigh so little on my mind as in the present case. In demanding a verdict of murder without extenuating circumstances, I am following not only the dictates of my conscience and a sacred obligation, but also those of the natural and righteous indignation I feel at the sight of a criminal devoid of the least spark of human feeling.'

When the prosecutor sat down there was a longish silence. Personally I was quite overcome by the heat and my amazement at what I had been hearing. The presiding judge gave a short cough, and asked me in a very low tone if I had anything to say. I rose, and as I felt in the mood to speak, I said the first thing that crossed my mind: that I'd had no intention of killing the Arab. The judge replied that this statement would be taken into consideration by the court. Meanwhile he would be glad to hear, before my counsel addressed the court, what were the motives of my crime. So far, he must admit, he hadn't fully understood the grounds of my defence.

I tried to explain that it was because of the sun, but I spoke too quickly and ran my words into each other. I was only too conscious that it sounded nonsensical, and, in fact, I heard people tittering.

My lawyer shrugged his shoulders. Then he was directed to address the court, in his turn. But all he did was to point out the lateness of the hour and to ask for an adjournment till the following afternoon. To this the judge agreed.

When I was brought back next day, the electric fans were still churning up the heavy air and the jurymen playing their gaudy little fans in a sort of steady rhythm. The speech for the defence seemed to me interminable. At one moment, however, I pricked up my ears; it was when I heard him saying: 'It is true I killed a man.' He went on in the same strain, saying 'I' when he referred to me. It seemed so queer that I bent towards the policeman on my right and asked him to explain. He told me to shut up; then, after a moment, whispered: 'They all do that.' It seemed to me that the idea behind it was still further to exclude me from the case, to put me off the map, so to speak, by substituting the lawyer for myself. Anyway, it hardly mattered; I already felt worlds away from this courtroom and its tedious 'proceedings'.

My lawyer, in any case, struck me as feeble to the point of being ridiculous. He hurried through his plea of provocation, and then he, too, started in about my 'soul'. But I had an impression that he had much less talent than the prosecutor.

'I, too,' he said, 'have closely studied this man's soul; but, unlike my learned friend for the prosecution, I have found something there. Indeed, I may say that I have read the prisoner's mind like an open book.' What he had read there was that I was an excellent young fellow, a steady, conscientious worker who did his best by his employer; that I was popular with everyone and sympathetic in others' troubles. According to him I was a dutiful son, who had supported his mother as long as he was able. After anxious consideration I had reached the conclusion that, by entering a Home, the old lady would have comforts that my means didn't permit me to provide for her. 'I am astounded, gentlemen,' he added, 'by the attitude taken up by my learned friend in referring to this Home. Surely if proof be needed of the excellence of such institutions, we need only remember that they are promoted and financed by a Government department.' I noticed that he made no reference to the funeral, and this seemed to me a serious omission. But, what with his long-windedness, the endless days and hours they had been discussing my 'soul', and the rest of it, I found that my mind had gone blurred; everything was dissolving into a greyish, watery haze.

Only one incident stands out; towards the end, while my counsel rambled on, I heard the tin trumpet of an ice-cream vendor in the street, a small, shrill sound cutting across the flow of words. And then a rush of memories went through my mind – memories of a life which was mine no longer and had once provided me with the surest, humblest pleasures: warm smells of summer, my favourite streets, the sky at evening, Marie's dresses and her laugh. The futility of what was happening here seemed to take me by the throat, I felt like vomiting, and I had only one idea: to get it over, to go back to my cell, and sleep . . . and sleep.

Dimly I heard my counsel making his last appeal.

'Gentlemen of the jury, surely you will not send to his death a decent, hard-working young man, because for one tragic moment he lost his self-control? Is he not sufficiently punished by the lifelong remorse that is to be his lot? I confidently await your verdict, the only verdict possible – that of homicide with extenuating circumstances.'

The court rose and the lawyer sat down, looking thoroughly exhausted. Some of his colleagues came to him and shook his hand. 'You put up a magnificent show, old chap,' I heard one of them say. Another lawyer even called me to witness: 'Fine, wasn't it?' I agreed, but insincerely; I was far too tired to judge if it had been 'fine' or otherwise.

Meanwhile the day was ending and the heat becoming less intense. By some vague sounds that reached me from the street I knew that the cool of the evening had set in. We all sat on, waiting. And what we all were waiting for really concerned nobody but me. I looked round the courtroom. It was exactly as it had been on the first day. I met the eyes of the journalist in grey and the robot woman. This reminded me that not once during the whole hearing had I tried to catch Marie's eye. It wasn't that I'd forgotten her; only I was too preoccupied. I saw her now, seated between Céleste and Raymond. She gave me a little wave of her hand, as if to say, 'At last!' She was smiling, but I could tell that she was rather anxious. But my heart seemed turned to stone, and I couldn't even return her smile.

The judges came back to their seats. Someone read out to the jury, very rapidly, a string of questions. I caught a word here and there. 'Murder of malice aforethought . . . Provocation . . . Extenuating circumstances.' The jury went out, and I was taken to the little room where I had already waited. My lawyer came to see me; he was very talkative and showed more cordiality and confidence than ever before. He assured me that all would go well and I'd get off with a few years' imprisonment or transportation. I asked him what were the chances of getting the sentence quashed. He said there was no chance of that. He had not raised any point of law, as this was apt to prejudice the jury. And it was difficult to get a judgement quashed except on technical grounds. I saw his point, and agreed. Looking at the matter dispassionately, I shared his view. Otherwise there would be no end to litigation. 'In any case,' the lawyer said, 'you can appeal in the ordinary way. But I'm convinced the verdict will be favourable.'

We waited for quite a while, a good three-quarters of an hour, I should say. Then a bell rang. My lawyer left me, saying:

'The foreman of the jury will read out the answers. You will be called on after that to hear the judgement.'

Some doors banged. I heard people hurrying down flights of steps, but couldn't tell whether they were near by or distant. Then I heard a voice droning away in the courtroom.

When the bell rang again and I stepped back into the dock, the silence of the courtroom closed in round me and, with the silence, came a queer sensation when I noticed that, for the first time, the young journalist kept his eyes averted. I didn't look in Marie's direction. In fact, I had no time to look as the presiding judge had already started pronouncing a rigmarole to the effect that 'in the name of the French People' I was to be decapitated in some public place.

It seemed to me then that I could interpret the look on the faces of those present; it was one of almost respectful sympathy. The policemen, too, handled me very gently. The lawyer placed his hand on my wrist. I had stopped thinking altogether. I heard the judge's voice asking if I had anything more to say. After thinking for a moment, I answered, 'No.' Then the policemen led me out.

5

I HAVE just refused, for the third time, to see the prison chaplain. I have nothing to say to him, don't feel like talking – and shall be seeing him quite soon enough, any-way. The only thing that interests me now is the problem of circumventing the machine, learning if the inevitable admits a loophole.

They have moved me to another cell. In this one, lying on my back, I can see the sky, and there is nothing else to see. All my time is spent in watching the slowly changing colours of the sky, as day moves on to night. I put my hands behind my head, gaze up, and wait.

This problem of a loophole obsesses me; I am always wondering if there have been cases of condemned prisoners escaping from the implacable machinery of justice at the last moment, breaking through the police cordon, vanishing in the nick of time before the guillotine falls. Often and often I blame myself for not having given more attention to accounts of public executions. One should always take an interest in such matters. There's never any knowing what one may come to. Like everyone else I'd read descriptions of executions in the papers. But technical books dealing with this subject must certainly exist; only I'd never felt sufficiently interested to look them up. And in these books I might have found escape stories. Surely they'd have told me that in one case anyhow the wheels had stopped; that once, if only once, in that inexorable march of events, chance or luck had played a happy part. Just once! In a way I think that single instance would have satisfied me. My emotion would have done the rest. The papers often talk of 'a debt owed to society' – a debt which, according to them, must be paid by the offender. But talk of that sort doesn't touch the imagination. No, the one thing that counted for me was the possibility of making a dash for it and defeating their blood-thirsty rite; of a mad stampede to freedom that would anyhow give me a moment's hope, the gambler's last throw. Naturally all that 'hope' could come to was to be knocked down at the corner of a street or picked off by a bullet in my back. But, all things considered, even this luxury was forbidden me; I was caught in the rat-trap irrevocably.

Try as I might, I couldn't stomach this brutal certitude. For really, when one came to think of it, there was a disproportion between the judgement on which it was based and the unalterable sequence of events starting from the moment when that judgement was delivered. The fact that the verdict was read out at 8 p.m. rather than at 5, the fact that it might have been quite different, that it was given by men who change their underclothes, and was credited to so vague an entity as the 'French People' – for that matter, why not to the Chinese or the German People? – all these facts seemed to deprive the court's decision of much of its gravity. Yet I could but recognize that, from the moment the verdict was given, its effects became as cogent, as tangible, as, for example, this wall against which I was lying, pressing my back to it.

When such thoughts crossed my mind, I remembered a story Mother used to tell me about my father. I never set eyes on him. Perhaps the only things I really knew about him were what Mother had told me. One of these was that he'd gone to see a murderer executed. The mere thought of it turned his stomach. But he'd seen it through and, on coming home, was violently sick. At the time I found my father's conduct rather disgusting. But now I understood; it was so natural. How had I failed to recognize that nothing was more important than an execution; that, viewed from one angle, it's the only thing that can genuinely interest a man? And I decided that, if ever I got out of gaol, I'd attend every execution that took place. I was unwise, no doubt, even to consider this possibility. For, the moment I'd pictured myself in freedom, standing behind a double rank of policemen – on the right side of the line, so to speak – the mere thought of being an onlooker who comes to see the show, and can go home and vomit afterwards, flooded my mind with a wild, absurd exultation. It was a stupid thing to let my imagination run away with me like that; a moment later I had a shivering fit and had to wrap myself closely in my blanket. But my teeth went on chattering; nothing would stop them.

Still, obviously, one can't be sensible all the time. Another equally ridiculous fancy of mine was to frame new laws, altering the penalties. What was wanted, to my mind, was to give the criminal a chance, if only a dog's chance; say, one chance in a thousand. There might be some drug, or combination of drugs, which would kill the patient (I thought of him as 'the patient') nine hundred and ninety times in a thousand. That he should know this was, of course, essential. For after taking much thought, calmly, I came to the conclusion that what was wrong about the guillotine was that the condemned man had no chance at all, absolutely none. In fact, the patient's death had been ordained irrevocably. It was a foregone conclusion. If by some fluke the knife didn't do its job, they started again. So it came to this, that – against the grain, no doubt – the condemned man had to hope the apparatus was in good working order ! This, I thought, was a flaw in the system; and, on the face of it, my view was sound enough. On the other hand, I had to admit it proved the efficiency of the system. It came to this: the man under sentence was obliged to collaborate mentally, it was in his interest that all should go off without a hitch.

Another thing I had to recognize was that, until now, I'd had wrong ideas on the subject. For some reason I'd always supposed that one had to go up steps and climb on to a scaffold to be guillotined. Probably that was because of the 1789 Revolution; I mean, what I'd learnt about it at school, and the pictures I had seen. Then one morning I remembered a photograph the newspapers had featured on the occasion of the execution of a famous criminal. Actually the apparatus stood on the ground; there was nothing very impressive about it, and it was much narrower than I'd imagined. It struck me as rather odd that picture had escaped my memory until now. What had struck me at the time was the neat appearance of the guillotine; its shining surfaces and finish reminded one of some laboratory instrument. One always has exaggerated ideas about what one doesn't know. Now I had to admit it seemed a very simple process, getting guillotined; the machine is on the same level as the man, and he walks towards it as one steps forward to meet some-body one knows. In a sense, that, too, was disappointing. The business of climbing a scaffold, leaving the world below one, so to speak, gave something for a man's imagination to get hold of. But, as it was, the machine dominated everything; they killed you discreetly, with a hint of shame and much efficiency.

There were two other things about which I was always thinking: the dawn, and my appeal. However, I did my best to keep my mind off these thoughts. I lay down, looked up at the sky, and forced myself to study it. When the light began to turn green I knew that night was coming. Another thing I did to deflect the course of my thoughts was to listen to my heart. I couldn't imagine that this faint throbbing, which had been with me for so long, would ever cease. Imagination has never been one of my strong points. Still, I tried to picture a moment when the beating of my heart no longer echoed in my head. But in vain. The dawn and my appeal were still there. And I ended by believing it was a silly thing to try to force one's thoughts out of their natural groove.

They always came for one at dawn; that much I knew. So really all my nights were spent in waiting for that dawn. I have never liked being taken by surprise. When something happens to me I want to be ready for it. That's why I got into the habit of sleeping off and on in the daytime and watching through the night for the first hint of daybreak in the dark dome above. The worst period of the night was that vague hour when, I knew, they usually came; once it was after midnight I waited, listening intently. Never before had my ears perceived so many noises, such tiny sounds. Still, I must say I was lucky in one respect; never during any of those periods did I hear footsteps. Mother used to say that however miserable one is, there's always something to be thankful for. And each morning, when the sky brightened and light began to flood my cell, I agreed with her. Because I might just as well have heard footsteps, and felt my heart shattered into bits. Even though the faintest rustle sent me hurrying to the door and, pressing an ear to the rough, cold wood, I listened so intently that I could hear my breathing, quick and hoarse like a dog's panting – even so there was an end; my heart hadn't split, and I knew I had another twenty-four hours' respite.

Then all day there was my appeal to think about. I made the most of this idea, studying my effects so as to squeeze out the maximum of consolation. Thus I always began by assuming the worst; my appeal was dismissed. That meant, of course, I was to die. Sooner than others, obviously. 'But', I reminded myself, 'it's common knowledge that life isn't worth living anyhow'. And, on a wide view, I could see that it makes little difference whether one dies at the age of thirty or three-score and ten – since, in either case, other men and women will continue living, the world will go on as before. Also, whether I died now or forty years hence, this business of dying had to be got through, inevitably. Still, somehow this line of thought wasn't as consoling as it should have been; the idea of all those years of life in hand was a galling reminder! However, I could argue myself out of it, by picturing what would have been my feelings when my term was up, and death had cornered me. Once one's up against it, the precise manner of one's death has obviously small importance. Therefore – but it was hard not to lose the thread of the argument leading up to that 'therefore' – I should be prepared to face the dismissal of my appeal.

At this stage, but only at this stage, I had, so to speak, the *right*, and accordingly I gave myself leave, to consider the other alternative; that my appeal was successful. And then the trouble was to calm down that sudden rush of joy racing through my body and even bringing tears to me eyes. But it was up to me to bring my nerves to heel and steady my mind; for, even in considering this possibility, I had to keep some order in my thoughts, so as to make my consolations, as regards the first alternative, more plausible. When I'd succeeded, I had earned a good hour's peace of mind; and that, anyhow, was something.

It was at one of these moments that I refused once again to see the chaplain. I was lying down and could mark the summer evening coming on by a soft golden glow spreading across the sky. I had just turned down my appeal, and felt my blood circulating with slow, steady throbs. No, I didn't want to see the chaplain. . . . Then I did something I hadn't done for quite a while; I fell to thinking about Marie. She hadn't written for ages; probably, I surmised, she had grown tired of being the mistress of a man sentenced to death. Or she might be ill, or dead. After all, such things happen. How could I have known about it, since, apart from our two bodies, separated now, there was no link between us, nothing to remind us of each other? Supposing she were dead, her memory would mean nothing; I couldn't feel an interest in a dead girl. This seemed to me quite normal; just as I realized people would soon forget me once I was dead. I couldn't even say that this was hard to stomach; really, there's no idea to which one doesn't get acclimatized in time.

My thoughts had reached this point when the chaplain walked in, unannounced. I couldn't help giving a start on seeing him. He noticed this evidently, as he promptly told me not to be alarmed. I reminded him that usually his visits were at another hour, and for a pretty grim occasion. This, he replied, was just a friendly visit; it had no concern with my appeal, about which he knew nothing. Then he sat down on my bed, asking me to sit beside him. I refused – not because I had anything against him; he seemed a mild, amiable man.

He remained quite still at first, his arms resting on his

knees, his eyes fixed on his hands. They were slender but sinewy hands, which made me think of two nimble little animals. Then he gently rubbed them together. He stayed so long in the same position that for a while I almost forgot he was there.

All of a sudden he jerked his head up and looked me in the eyes.

'Why', he asked, 'don't you let me come to see you?'

I explained that I didn't believe in God.

'Are you really so sure of that?'

I said I saw no point in troubling my head about the matter; whether I believed or didn't was, to my mind, a question of so little importance.

He then leant back against the wall, laying his hands flat on his thighs. Almost without seeming to address me, he remarked that he'd often noticed one fancies one is quite sure about something, when in point of fact one isn't. When I said nothing he looked at me again, and asked:

'Don't you agree?'

I said that seemed quite possible. But, though I mightn't be so sure about what interested me, I was absolutely sure about what didn't interest me. And the question he had raised didn't interest me at all.

He looked away and, without altering his posture, asked if it was because I felt utterly desperate that I spoke like this. I explained that it wasn't despair I felt, but fear – which was natural enough.

'In that case,' he said firmly, 'God can help you. All the men I've seen in your position turned to Him in their time of trouble.'

Obviously, I replied, they were at liberty to do so, if they felt like it. I however, didn't want to be helped, and I hadn't time to work up interest for something that didn't interest me.

He fluttered his hands fretfully; then, sitting up, smoothed out his cassock. When this was done he began talking again, addressing me as 'my friend'. It wasn't because I'd been condemned to death, he said, that he spoke to me in this way. In his opinion every man on the earth was under sentence of death.

There, I interrupted him; that wasn't the same thing, I pointed out, and, what's more, could be no consolation.

He nodded. 'Maybe. Still, if you don't die soon, you'll die one day. And then the same question will arise. How will you face that terrible, final hour?'

I replied that I'd face it exactly as I was facing it now.

Thereat he stood up, and looked me straight in the eyes. It was a trick I knew well. I used to amuse myself trying it on Emmanuel and Céleste and nine times out of ten they'd look away uncomfortably. I could see the chaplain was an old hand at it, as his gaze never faltered. And his voice was quite steady when he said: 'Have you no hope at all? Do you really think that when you die you die outright, and nothing remains?'

I said: 'Yes.'

He dropped his eyes and sat down again. He was truly sorry for me, he said. It must make life unbearable for a man, to think as I did.

The priest was beginning to bore me, and, resting a shoulder on the wall, just beneath the little skylight, I looked away. Though I didn't trouble much to follow what he said, I gathered he was questioning me again. Presently his tone became agitated, urgent, and, as I realized that he was genuinely distressed, I began to pay more attention.

He said he felt convinced my appeal would succeed, but I was saddled with a load of guilt, of which I must get rid. In his view man's justice was a vain thing; only God's justice mattered. I pointed out that the former had condemned me. Yes, he agreed, but it hadn't absolved me from my sin. I told him that I wasn't conscious of any 'sin'; all I knew was that I'd been guilty of a criminal offence. Well, I was paying the penalty of that offence, and no one had the right to expect anything more of me.

Just then he got up again, and it struck me that if he wanted to move in this tiny cell, almost the only choice lay between standing up and sitting down. I was staring at the floor. He took a single step towards me, and halted, as if he didn't dare to come nearer. Then he looked up through the bars at the sky.

'You're mistaken, my son,' he said gravely. 'There's more that might be required of you. And perhaps it *will* be required of you.'

'What do you mean?'

'You might be asked to see . . .'

'To see what?'

Slowly the priest gazed round my cell, and I was struck by the sadness of his voice when he spoke again.

'These stone walls, I know it only too well, are steeped in human suffering. I've never been able to look at them without a shudder. And yet – believe me, I am speaking from the depths of my heart – I *know* that even the wretchedest among you have sometimes seen, taking form upon that greyness, a divine face. It's that face you are asked to see.'

This roused me a little. I informed him that I'd been staring at those walls for months; there was nobody, nothing in the world, I knew better than I knew them. And once upon a time, perhaps, I used to try to see a face. But it was a sun-gold face, glowing with desire – Marie's face. I had no luck; I'd never seen it, and now I'd given up trying. Indeed I'd never seen anything 'taking form', as he called it, against those grey walls.

The chaplain gazed at me mournfully. I now had my back to the wall and light was flowing over my forehead. He muttered some words I didn't catch; then abruptly asked if he might kiss me. I said, 'No.' Then he turned, came up to the wall, and slowly drew his hand along it.

'Do you really love these earthly things so very much?' he asked in a low voice.

I made no reply.

For quite a while he kept his eyes averted. His presence was getting more and more irksome, and I was on the point of telling him to go, and leave me in peace, when all of a sudden he swung round on me, and burst out passionately:

'No! No! I refuse to believe it. I'm sure you've often wished there was an after-life.'

Of course I had, I told him. Everybody has that wish at times. But that had no more importance than wishing to be rich, or to swim very fast, or to have a better-shaped mouth. It was in the same order of things. I was going on in the same vein, when he cut in with a question. How did I picture my life after the grave?

I fairly bawled out at him: 'A life in which I can remember this life on earth. That's all I want of it.' And in the same breath I told him I'd had enough of his company.

But, apparently, he had more to say on the subject of God. I went close up to him and made a last attempt to explain that I'd very little time left, and I wasn't going to waste it on God.

Then he tried to change the subject by asking me why I hadn't once addressed him as 'Father', seeing that he was a priest. That irritated me still more, and I told him he wasn't my father; quite the contrary, he was on the others' side.

'No, no, my son,' he said, laying his hand on my shoulder.

'I'm on *your* side, though you don't realize it – because your heart is hardened. But I shall pray for you.'

Then, I don't know how it was, but something seemed to break inside me, and I started yelling at the top of my voice. I hurled insults at him, I told him not to waste his rotten prayers on me; it was better to burn than to disappear. I'd taken him by the neckband of his cassock, and, in a sort of ecstasy of joy and rage, I poured out on him all the thoughts that had been simmering in my brain. He seemed so cocksure, you see. And yet none of his certainties was worth one strand of a woman's hair. Living as he did, like a corpse, he couldn't even be sure of being alive. It might look as if my hands were empty. Actually, I was sure of myself, sure about everything, far surer than he; sure of my present life and of the death that was coming. That, no doubt, was all I had; but at least that certainty was something I could get my teeth into – just as it had got its teeth into me. I'd been right, I was still right, I was always right. I'd passed my life in a certain way, and I might have passed it in a different way, if I'd felt like it. I'd acted thus, and I hadn't acted otherwise; I hadn't done *x*, whereas I had done *y* or *z*. And what did that mean? That, all the time, I'd been waiting for this present moment, for that dawn, tomorrow's or another day's, which was to justify me. Nothing, nothing had the least importance, and I knew quite well why. He, too, knew why. From the dark horizon of my future a sort of slow, persistent breeze had been blowing towards me, all my life long, from the years that were to come. And on its way that breeze had levelled out all the ideas that people tried to foist on me in the equally unreal years I then was living through. What difference could they make to me, the death of others, or a mother's love, or his God; or the way one decides to live, the fate one thinks one chooses, since one and the same fate was bound to 'choose' not only me but thousands of millions of privileged people who, like him, called themselves my brothers. Surely, surely he must see that? Every man alive was privileged; there was only one class of men, the privileged class. All alike would be condemned to die one day; his turn, too, would come like the others'. And what difference could it make if, after being charged with murder, he were executed because he didn't weep at his mother's funeral, since it all came to the same thing in the end? The same thing for Salamano's wife and for Salamano's dog. That little robot woman was as 'guilty' as the girl from Paris who had married Masson, or as Marie, who wanted me to marry her. What did it matter if Raymond was as much my pal as Céleste, who was a far worthier man? What did it matter if at this very moment Marie was kissing a new boy friend? As a condemned man himself, couldn't he grasp what I meant by that dark wind blowing from my future? . . .

I had been shouting so much that I'd lost my breath, and just then the warders rushed in and started trying to release the chaplain from my grip. One of them made as if to strike me. The chaplain quietened them down, and gazed at me for a moment without speaking. I could see tears in his eyes. Then he turned and left the cell.

Once he'd gone, I felt calm again. But all this excitement had exhausted me and I dropped heavily on to my sleeping-plank. I must have had a longish sleep, for, when I woke, the stars were shining down on my face. Sounds of the countryside came faintly in, and the cool night air, veined with smells of earth and salt, fanned my cheeks. The marvellous peace of the sleepbound summer night flooded through me like a tide. Then, just on the edge of daybreak, I heard a steamer's siren. People were starting on a voyage to a world which had ceased to concern me, for ever. Almost for the first time in many months I thought of my

119

mother. And now, it seemed to me, I understood why at her life's end she had taken on a 'fiancé'; why she'd played at making a fresh start. There, too, in that Home where lives were flickering out, the dusk came as a mournful solace. With death so near, Mother must have felt like someone on the brink of freedom, ready to start life all over again. No one, no one in the world had any right to weep for her. And I, too, felt ready to start life over again. It was as if that great rush of anger had washed me clean, emptied me of hope, and, gazing up at the dark sky spangled with its signs and stars, for the first time, the first, I laid my heart open to the benign indifference of the universe. To feel it so like myself, indeed so brotherly, made me realize that I'd been happy, and that I was happy still. For all to be accomplished, for me to feel less lonely, all that remained was to hope that on the day of my execution there should be a huge crowd of spectators and that they should greet me with howls of execration.

MORE ABOUT PENGUINS

Penguin Book News, an attractively illustrated magazine which appears every month, contains details of all the new books issued by Penguins as they are published. Every four months it is supplemented by *Penguins in Print*, which is a complete list of all books published by Penguins which are still available. (There are well over two thousand of these.)

A specimen copy of *Penguin Book News* can be sent to you free on request, and you can become a regular subscriber at 3s for twelve issues (with the complete lists). Just write to Dept EP, Penguin Books Ltd, Harmondsworth, Middlesex, enclosing a cheque or postal order, and your name will be added to the mailing list.

Some other books published by Penguins are described on the following pages.

Note: *Penguin Book News* and *Penguins in Print*
are not available in the U.S.A. or Canada

ALBERT CAMUS
The Plague

When Albert Camus was killed in a road accident early in 1960, the *Guardian* critic Anthony Hartley described his death as a 'terrible blow to French Literature' and to those who admire . . . 'the limpid, upright mind which is reflected in all his work . . .'

The Plague, which won Camus the Prix des Critiques in 1947, is considered by many to have been his finest book. In an obituary notice *The Times* described it as 'a carefully wrought metaphysical novel the machinery of which can be compared to a Sophoclean tragedy. The plague in question afflicted Oran in the 1940s; and on one plane the book is a straightforward narrative. Into it, however, can be read all Camus's native anxieties, centred on the idea of plague as a symbol.' The symbol is that of the German occupation of France against which Camus fought so heroically during the war.

This is a magnificent and impressive book, which by the nature of its theme is often horrifying but never horrific, and which expresses most clearly the author's basic humanitarianism.

Also available

THE FALL*

NOT FOR SALE IN THE U.S.A.
*NOT FOR SALE IN THE U.S.A. OR CANADA

ALBERT CAMUS

Exile and the Kingdom

These six short stories show the same qualities that won a Nobel Prize for Literature for the late Albert Camus. Four of them are set in Algeria on the fringes of the desert – an environment which has often been associated with deep mystical and emotional experience. 'The Renegade' shows the great French novelist at his most intense, as he disturbingly uncovers the slave mentality of a missionary, reduced by torture to treachery. On the other hand 'The Artist at Work' is a gay and ludicrous satire on the pitfalls of artistic success.

'Such is the evocation of atmosphere and scene that . . . one is forced on stage to suffer vicariously with the hapless characters . . . These are powerful, jolting, thought-provoking parables, told skilfully and with detached passion' – *Sunday Times*

'These violent yet controlled stories confirm . . . that Camus is no simple, superficial humanitarian. He is on the side of the angels, as he should be, but he gives the devil a very good run for his money' – *Observer*

NOT FOR SALE IN THE U.S.A. OR CANADA

ALBERT CAMUS

The Rebel

'It is not only the best book Camus has written, but one of the vital works of our time, compassionate and disillusioned, intelligent but instructed by deeply felt experience' – *Observer* profile

Camus himself described this work as 'an attempt to understand the time I live in'. 'One might think,' he continues, 'that a period which, within fifty years, uproots, enslaves or kills seventy million human beings, should only, and forthwith, be condemned. But also its guilt must be understood.

'Slave camps under the flag of freedom, massacres justified by philanthropy or the taste for the superhuman, cripple judgement. On the day when crime puts on the apparel of innocence, through a curious reversal peculiar to our age, it is innocence that is called on to justify itself. The purpose of this essay is to accept and study that strange challenge.'

JEAN-PAUL SARTRE

The Age of Reason

This novel by one of France's greatest post-war writers covers two days in the life of Mathieu Delarue, a teacher of philosophy, and in the lives of his acquaintances and friends. Mathieu is trying to raise money for the abortion of a woman with whom he has been living for seven years, and at the same time he is obsessed with a desire for personal freedom. Individual tragedies, and happiness, are etched against the Paris summer of 1938, with its night clubs, galleries, students, and café society.

But behind it all there is a threat, only half realized at the time, of the coming catastrophe of the Second World War.

'There is a wonderful feeling of suspense about the book' – Henry Reed in the *Listener*

'Constantly delights with its brilliance' – *Spectator*

'A dynamic, deeply disturbing novel' – Elizabeth Bowen

NOT FOR SALE IN THE U.S.A.

JEAN-PAUL SARTRE

The Reprieve

The Reprieve follows *The Age of Reason* in Sartre's tetralogy, *Roads to Freedom*, and includes many of the characters of the first book. It surveys that heat-wave week in September 1938 when Europe waited tensely for the result of the Munich conference. Sartre's technique of almost simultaneous description of several scenes enables him to suggest this mood of all Europe as it tried hard to blinker itself against the threat of war. And this particular situation, realized in depth and historical detail, is made to typify universal human characteristics, such as man's tendency to try to avoid positive action – to hope against hope for a Reprieve.

'His method is consummately able. It is only a writer with an exquisite sense of rhythm who can mix episode with episode as M. Sartre does here' – *Observer*

'In richness, imaginative scope, and clarity of observation, it is . . . a feat of a rare, perhaps of a unique kind' – *Listener*

Also available

IRON IN THE SOUL

NAUSEA

NOT FOR SALE IN THE U.S.A.

SIMONE DE BEAUVOIR

She Came to Stay

Written as an act of revenge against the woman who once so nearly disrupted her life with the philosopher Jean-Paul Sartre, Simone de Beauvoir's first novel is a brilliant success in its own right – a passionate and ironic work of art.

Also available

MEMOIRS OF A DUTIFUL DAUGHTER

THE PRIME OF LIFE

FORCE OF CIRCUMSTANCE

THE BLOOD OF OTHERS

NOT FOR SALE IN THE U.S.A.

Crick, Watson
& DNA

PAUL STRATHERN

ARROW

Published in the United Kingdom in 1997 by
Arrow Books

5 7 9 10 8 6 4

First published in the United Kingdom
in 1997 by Arrow Books

Arrow Books Limited
Random House UK Ltd
20 Vauxhall Bridge Road, London SW1V 2SA

Random House Australia (Pty) Limited
20 Alfred Street, Milsons Point, Sydney,
New South Wales 2061, Australia

Random House New Zealand Limited
18 Poland Road, Glenfield
Auckland 10, New Zealand

Random House South Africa (Pty) Limited
Endulini, 5a Jubilee Road, Parktown 2193, South Africa

Random House UK Limited Reg. No. 954009

A CIP catalogue record for this book
is available from the British Library

Papers used by Random House UK Limited are natural,
recyclable products made from wood grown in sustainable
forests. The manufacturing processes conform to the en-
vironmental regulations of the country of origin

Typeset in Bembo by SX Composing DTP, Rayleigh, Essex
Printed and bound in the United Kingdom by
Cox & Wyman Ltd, Reading, Berkshire.

ISBN 0 09 923742 3

CONTENTS

INTRODUCTION

The great scientific advance of the first half of the 20th century was nuclear physics. Relativity and quantum theory began unlocking the secrets of the atom, discovering the ultimate matter of the universe. Nuclear physics became the cutting edge of human knowledge.

The mid-century discovery of the structure of DNA created an entirely new science. This was molecular biology, which began unlocking the secrets of life itself. Molecular biology now became the nuclear physics of the second half of the 20th century.

The discoveries being made in this field (and the possible discoveries yet to be made) are transforming our entire conception of life. Like children, we have discovered the ultimate building blocks of life, and we are also learning how they can be taken apart. Once again, science has outstripped morality. We are acquiring dangerous knowledge, without any clear idea of how we should use it. As yet, we are barely grappling with the moral problems posed by nuclear physics (which may yet destroy us). Molecular biology is showing us how to transform life into almost anything.

Such scary possibilities were barely glimpsed by those who sought to discover 'the secret of life'. For them, this was one of the great scientific adventures. This adventure may have been pure in its aims, but those who took part in it were not immune from human frailty. All human life is here: ambition, supreme intelligence, folly, wishful thinking, incompetence, and sheer luck (both good and bad) – all had their part to play. The search for the secret of life proved no different from life itself. And the answer, when it was finally discovered, fell into the same category. The structure of DNA is fiendishly complex, astonishingly beautiful, and contains the seeds of tragedy.

ON THE WAY TO DNA: A HISTORY OF GENETICS

Until little over a century ago, genetics was mostly old wives' tales. People saw what happened, but had no idea how or why it happened.

References to genetics go back as far as biblical times. According to Genesis, Jacob had a method for making sure that his sheep and goats gave birth to spotted and speckled offspring. He did this by making them breed in front of sticks with strips of peeled bark which had a similar mottled effect.

More realistically, the Babylonians understood that for a date palm to be fruitful, pollen from the male palm had to be introduced to the pistils of the female palm.

The ancient Greek philosophers were the first to look at the world in a recognisably scientific fashion. As a result they produced theories about almost everything, and genetics was no exception. Aristotle's observations led him to conclude that the male and female do not make equal contributions to their offspring. Their contributions are qualitatively different: the female gives 'matter', the male gives 'motion'.

A prevalent belief in ancient times held that if a female had previously mated and had progeny, the characteristics of their father would appear in the woman's subsequent progeny by any other male. This fairy story was even dignified with a pseudo-scientific name by the ancient Greeks, who called it telegony (meaning 'distant-begetting').

A more interesting theory was pangenesis, which held that each organ and substance of the body secreted its own particles, which then combined to form the embryo.

Such beliefs recur in genetic theory through the centuries, in a manner curiously similar to the actual recurrence of genetic traits. (Pangenesis was to pop up for well over 2000 years, and was even accepted by Darwin.)

Biology, and with it genetics, crossed the threshold into science in the 17th century. This was almost entirely due to the microscope, which was invented by the Dutch lens-grinder and counterfeiter Zacharias Jansen in the early 1600s. Microscopes led to the discovery of the cell. (This term was first used by the British physicist Robert Hooke, but was in fact misapplied to the tiny *spaces* left by dead cells, which reminded him of prison cells.)

The discovery of sex cells (or germ cells) caused great excitement. Soon over-enthusiastic microscopists were convinced that they had observed 'homunculi' (tiny human forms) inside the cells, and it looked as if the problem of reproduction was solved. More importantly, the English botanist Nehemiah Grew speculated that plants and animals were 'contrivances of the same wisdom'. He suggested that plants too have sexual organs and exhibit sexual behaviour. When the pioneer Swedish biologist Carl Linnaeus introduced his classification for species of plants and animals, the way was opened for more systematic research. The study of hybrids led to further speculation about the nature of genetic material.

For centuries it had been widely accepted that heredity was transmitted by 'blood'. (Hence the origin of such commonplace expressions as 'blue blood', 'blood line', 'mixed blood' and so forth.) This was not only loose, but inadequate. How could the same parents produce differing off-spring from the same 'blood'? Also, what accounted for the appearance of characteristics not present in either parent, but seen in long-dead ancestors and distant relatives? For instance, in thoroughbred racehorse breeding, piebalds have been known to recur after a gap of *dozens* of generations. (This example reveals one of the great lost opportunities of genetics. All English thoroughbreds are descended from the 43 'Royal Mares' imported by Charles II, and three orien-tal stallions imported a few years earlier. The breeding books trace each blood-line back to its origins, with notes on the characteristics of each progeny. Well over a century before genetics was born, any Newmarket trainer had at his fingertips sufficient material to found this science.)

By the mid-18th century the scientists had at last started speculating along lines that were obvi-ous to any racehorse breeder. The idea of evolu-tion began to circulate. One of the early developers of this idea was the 18th century philosopher–poet–scientist Erasmus Darwin (grandfather of the famous Charles). Erasmus Darwin was convinced that species were capable of change. Any creature with 'lust, hunger and a desire for security' would organically adapt to its surroundings. But how?

The French naturalist Jean Lamarck came up with the first coherent theory of evolution. Lamarck had been born in 1744, the son of a broke aristo. By the age of 37 he had become Botanist to the King. When the Revolution took place Louis XVI was executed, along with any blue-blood who could be found. But Lamarck quickly evolved a suitable social cover, and emerged as Professor of Zoology at Paris. In the light of such experience, it's not surprising that Lamarck believed in the effect of environment on evolution.

According to Lamarck, 'acquired characteristics are inherited'. In other words, a man who has learned how to become a skilful fencer will pass on this skill to his son. This sounds fairly plausible – especially when one considers the Bach family. A son often does exhibit certain characteristics acquired by his father. But not for

Lamarck's reason. The fencer son may have inherited his father's athleticism and quick-wittedness, but not his *actual skill*. The fault in the 'acquired characteristics' theory is demonstrated by a more extreme example: even after generations of being blinded at birth to work in coal mines, pit ponies were still not born blind. Nevertheless, not long after Lamarck died the idea of evolution gradually became more widespread. (To this day, there is a statue of Lamarck in the Luxembourg Gardens in Paris, inscribed 'the inventor of evolution'.)

The father of evolution received little recognition during his lifetime, but the father of genetics received none. Gregor Mendel was born in 1822 in Silesia, which was then part of the Austro-Hungarian Empire. His parents were peasants and he was forced to abandon university because he had no money. In order to continue his studies he entered the priesthood, where he taught himself science yet failed his simple teaching exams. Allegedly this was because of 'examination amnesia', though the fact that he scored lowest marks in biology speaks of some more profound resistance to systemised knowledge.

Despite this, it was in systemisation that Mendel showed his genius. Mendel ended up at a monastery just outside Bruno, in what is now the Czech Republic. Put to work in the monastery garden, he began a long and systematic series of experiments cross-breeding edible pea plants (*pisum*). Mendel studied seven different characters of the plants, such as flower colour, height, seed shapes and so forth. He found, for instance, that if tall plants were crossed with short plants, the result was tall plants. But when these first generation hybrids were crossed with each other, they produced 75% tall plants and 25% short plants.

Mendel concluded that each character was determined by two 'factors', one contributed by each parent plant. For instance, the character height was determined by a 'tallness' factor and a 'shortness' factor. The 'tallness' factor and the 'shortness' factor both remained in the plants. They did not blend, they retained their separate identities – but one was dominant. In this case the 'tallness' factor was dominant. This explained why when the plants were initially crossed, their hybrid offspring were all tall. But when the hybrids were crossed, the 'tallness' and 'shortness' factors split and reformed.

Each parent contributes one factor to each off-spring, producing four possible combinations:

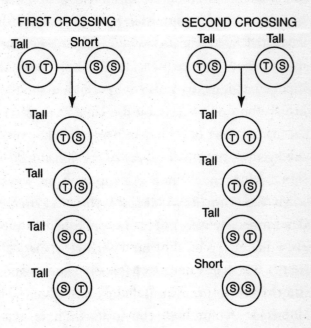

This accounted for the 75% : 25% distribution of tall plants and short plants after the second crossing.

Mendel's 'factors' are basically what we now call genes. It looked as if genes held the key to heredity. After conducting over 20,000 experiments Mendel came to further conclusions. Firstly, plants inherited an equal amount of 'factors' (or genes) from each parent. Also, separated pairs of genes always paired up again independently of one another. He further suggested that these genes were transmitted by germ cells.

Mendel had indicated why certain observable characteristics (such as piebaldness in horses) could skip generations, and also why children of the same parents do not exhibit the same characteristics (because the independent pairing of the separated genes produces a variety of combinations).

In 1866 Mendel finished a paper on his work called 'Experiments with Plant Hybrids' (*Versuche über Pflanzenhybriden*). This he published in the magazine of the local Natural Science Society at Bruno. The paper outlines Mendel's experiments and the brilliant statistical deductions which led him to his revolutionary conclusions. These conclusions – now known as Mendel's Laws – were to be the foundation of modern genetics.

But this lay years in the future. Not surprisingly, few leading scientists studied the pages of the Bruno Natural Science Society magazine.

For the moment no one was interested in Mendel's revolutionary findings; so he sent his paper to the top German botanist von Naegeli, at the University of Munich. Unfortunately Naegeli clung to the quaint belief in spontaneous generation. In his view, biological elements were created spontaneously by nature at cell level, and these elements then combined to produce pure species. The creation of species thus came about for no apparent reason, at the spontaneous whim of nature. According to this theory hybrids were mere freaks, and Mendel's experimental evidence was therefore irrelevant.

Despite Mendel's years of painstaking research, Naegeli told him that he needed to conduct yet more experiments if he was to convince anyone with his findings. Naegeli suggested that this time he should use hawkweed (*Hieracium*). Sadly hawkweed was an exceptional case, and Mendel's results did not match his previous findings. Mendel became somewhat disillusioned, and around the same time was elected abbot of his monastery. There was little time for further experiments on his previous exhaustive scale, and he died without recognition in 1884.

Not until 1900 did Mendel's work come to light. Only then, 34 years after the publication of his original paper, did he receive the universal acclaim he deserved. But such widespread renown can have its drawbacks. In 1936 Mendel's findings were scrutinised by the British scientist Sir Ronald Fisher, pioneer of modern statistics, who found that Mendel had committed the unforgiveable scientific sin. On a number of occasions Mendel had fudged his figures to make his statistics fit his thesis. Fortunately the science of genetics was by this stage well and truly launched, with no chance of being sunk by this pedagogic depth-charge. (Modern genetics is not alone here. Margaret Mead, the mother of modern anthropology, established herself as the world leader in her field when she published *Coming of Age in Samoa* in 1928. Not until many years later, by which time anthropology had built a firm structure on this foundation, was it discovered that many of Mead's colourful and optimistic findings in this work were sheer fantasy. But anthropology, like genetics, was far too well-established to be sunk by mere facts.)

Mendel had conclusively disproved the 'blood'

theory of heredity – which implied that the characteristics of parents are blended in their offspring. But as his work remained unknown, this theory continued to flourish. Even Charles Darwin believed that heredity was transmitted in this fashion. He also accepted telegony – having witnessed a case where a mare, who had previously mated with a zebra, gave birth to a foal with stripes after mating with an Arab stallion. And unlike Mead or Mendel, Darwin had a scrupulous regard for the facts. We can only assume that he was hoodwinked by a cunning zebra owner, or one of the horses had a striped ancestor.

Fortunately Darwin's work in the related field of heredity was to prove more lasting. The publication of his *The Origin of Species* in 1859 introduced the idea of 'the survival of the fittest'. Species evolved by natural selection. The entire history of life on earth appeared to be explained.

Despite this, the French Lamarckists continued to believe in the inheritance of acquired characteristics. According to them, the giraffe had grown its long neck as a result of generations continually stretching for high leaves. This theory was to be conclusively disproved in the 1890s by the heartless German biologist August Weismann, who must have been deeply impressed by nursery rhymes in his childhood. Evoking scenes from 'Three Blind Mice', he conducted experiments in which he amputated the tails of mice for several generations. Despite this grim practice, the mice's tails neither disappeared nor became shorter. Weismann drew an important conclusion: hereditary inheritance is carried by germ cells (sex cells), and is not influenced by what happens to the organism.

That other persistent myth, the blood theory, was finally laid to rest by Darwin's cousin Francis Galton. In another series of unfeeling but apparently vital experiments, Galton transfused blood from white rabbits into black rabbits. The rabbits may have felt as if they were turning green, but in fact the transfusions had no effect. When the black rabbits were well enough to resume their normal activities, it was found that none of their numerous progeny had white fur. Heredity was certainly not transmitted by blood.

Darwin may have explained what happened to hereditary characteristics, but how these were actually conveyed from generation to generation remained a mystery. Weismann and Galton had conclusively demonstrated that this happened at cell level. More importantly, Mendel had shown that the information was carried by 'factors' (genes) – but this information still languished in a back number of the Bruno Natural Science Society magazine.

Meanwhile advances had been made in a field which for the moment appeared to have little relevance to genetics. In 1869 the 25-year-old Swiss biochemist Friedrich Miescher was researching at Tübingen into the composition of white blood cells. For his source material he used bandages from the operating theatre of a local hospital – a rich source of pus, whose main ingredient is white blood cells. By adding hydrochloric acid solution, he was able to obtain pure nuclei. He then stripped these down still further by adding alkali, then acid. In the process he obtained a grey precipitate quite different from any previously known organic substance. He named this nuclein – since it was part of the nucleus. This we now know as DNA.

Ten years later the German pioneer of cell

structure research, Walther Flemming, began using the newly discovered analine dyes to stain the nuclei of cells. He discovered that these dyes imparted colour to a band-like structure within the nucleus. This he named chromatin (from the Greek *chroma*, meaning colour). A couple of years later it was discovered that nuclein and chromatin reacted in precisely the same way: they appeared to contain the same substance. Chromatin consists of what we now call (after it) chromosomes, which in turn contain nuclein – or DNA. And DNA is what makes up the genes discovered by Mendel. All the disparate pieces were beginning to come together.

However, we can only see this in hindsight. At the time, these developments were disparate. Those involved didn't know where their work was leading them – even if they did have immediate aims (such as discovering cell structure or understanding the patterns of heredity). Only when the connection between these developments was made would the further picture emerge.

As early as the 1870s the German biologist Oskar Hertwig had made an important discovery whilst studying sea urchins under the recently developed light microscope. During fertilization sperm penetrated the egg, and the nuclei of the sperm fused with the nuclei of the egg. The importance of chromatin (chromosomes) in this fertilization process quickly became apparent when the Belgian embryologist Edouard van Beneden began studying an intestinal thread-worm found in horses, called *Ascaris megalo-cephala*. This big-headed parasite had only a few, large chromosomes, which made for easier observation. Beneden found that the sperm and the egg both contributed the same number of chromosomes in the fertilization process. He also discovered that there is a constant number of chromosomes per cell, which varies according to the species. (The threadworm, for instance, has just four chromosomes per cell, whereas the human cell contains 46.)

But if the nuclei of the sperm and the nuclei of the egg both contained an equal amount of chro-mosomes, and both contributed an equal amount of chromosomes, the amount of chromosomes should *double* during fertilization. Beneden noticed that this did not happen. Instead the chromosome number remained constant, maintaining the characteristic number for the species. This process, by which the number of chromosomes halves in the germ cells (formed by the egg and the sperm), Beneden called meiosis, from the Greek 'to decrease'. Meiosis was eventually explained by Flemming, the original discoverer of chromatin. He noticed that instead of merging directly the chromosome groups split lengthways into identical halves. These scattered through the cell, and *then* merged with each other. Here, at cell level, was a process which bore an uncanny resemblance to the splitting of 'factors' described by Mendel.

During the early years of the 20th century the American experimenter Thomas Hunt Morgan became aware of this resemblance; but he was unconvinced by Mendel's findings. Morgan, a great grandson of the man who had composed the US national anthem, undertook an exhaustive series of experiments breeding fruit flies (*Drosophila*). These flies have a life cycle of just 14 days, allowing for rapid statistical work. Despite encountering discrepancies with Mendel's findings (which were nothing to do with Mendel's occasional fudging), Morgan was eventually convinced that Mendel had been on the right track.

Extending Mendel's work on 'factors' (genes), Morgan showed that *Drosophila* had four groups of linked genes. The fact that some genes frequently remained together from generation to generation suggested a linking mechanism. Morgan decided that they could only be joined together on chromosomes. As there were four groups of genes, he concluded that *Drosophila* had four chromosomes.

Further statistical work showed that the assortment of *Drosophila* characters did not follow Mendel's laws. This could be accounted for by the splitting and recombining of chromosomes which Flemming had already observed. The splitting allowed some genes on the same chromosome to reassort, whereas others remained linked. This meant that genes at a greater distance from one another on the chomosome were more likely to reassort. And the higher the frequency of reassortment, the further apart the genes. Morgan realised that genes could be mapped.

In 1911 Morgan produced the first chromosome map, indicating the relative location of five sex-linked genes. Just over a decade later he had extended this map to include the relative positions of over 2000 genes on *Drosophila's* four chromosomes. Things were moving fast.

They began to move even faster when one of Morgan's students discovered a method of increasing the mutation rate of *Drosophila*. Hermann Müller discovered that when the flies were irradiated with X-rays, they produced mutations at 150 times their normal rate. They also produced mutations which didn't occur in nature. Weird hybrids with deformed wings and misshapen sexual organs began to appear. This led Müller to conclude that X-rays caused a reaction between chemicals in the genes. Essentially, mutation seemed to be the result of a chemical reaction.

Müller's joy at this vital discovery was tempered by a grim realization. Science was moving forward without control. The legend of Frankenstein producing monsters in his laboratory was coming true. X-rays could also be used to produce mutant human beings.

Genetics was becoming aware of its inherent dangers. Discoveries in this field were discoveries about the secrets of life itself. They revealed how it passed from generation to generation, and how it *changed*. What was known could also be used.

For the time being the possibility of isolating the gene remained remote. All that scientists could observe, even through the most powerful microscope, was the dim shadow of the chromosome. Where genes were concerned, science was still feeling forward into the dark. But Müller's demonstration of how to increase mutation meant that the gene's properties could now be extensively analysed. We might not have been able to see the gene, but we could find out what was there.

Müller's X-ray experiments made him famous, and in 1932 he took up a post in Berlin. A year later, a dangerous human mutation (not, as far as we know, arising from X-ray irradiation) took over the political reins in Germany. Neither Hitler's gene structure, nor his views on genetics, appealed to Müller and he left the country. Alas, Müller merely exchanged the frying pan for the fire. He now moved to Stalinist Russia.

By coincidence, Müller here encountered the second extra-scientific issue which 20th century genetics would be forced to confront. Communism was creating the world of the future; social engineering was seen as a science – and vice versa. But things are not as easy as this.

Ultimately, the direction science takes will always be a matter of human choice. (We found out how to leave the planet, rather than clean up the mess we'd made of it.) Science may follow human wishes, but it does not *conform* to them. In communist Russia, it was expected to do so – at least where genetics was concerned.

Soon after Müller arrived, top Russian geneticists began to 'disappear' because they did not subscribe to the prevailing theory. This was peddled by a crafty and ambitious charlatan called Trofim Lysenko, who claimed to believe in Lamarckism. The idea that the heredity of organisms (including human beings) could be influenced by their environment (such as society) had an obvious appeal to scientific thinkers of Stalin's calibre. Acquired characteristics (such as communist beliefs) could be inherited, and a new type of human being altogether would emerge in the coming utopia.

Lysenko's ideas were to render Russian

biology a laughing stock for *30 years* (1934-64). During this period serious scientists were expected to believe that wheat raised under suitable conditions could produce rye seed, and similar tall stories. (By corollary, domestic pussycats evicted to live in the wild would produce tigers – which must have made soviet citizens somewhat wary of stray cats.) Müller argued that such nonsense was utterly disproved by X-ray irradiation. Flies subjected to this also produced 'natural' mutations – proving that they were the result of inner chemical changes, which were nothing to do with insect society. Müller eventually returned to the United States, where he became an active campaigner against the abuse of science, as well as its own abuses.

Heredity was transferred by chemical reaction, but how did this work? When analysed, the gene-bearing chromosome was found to contain a number of different proteins and nucleic acids. Either one, or a combination of these, was evidently the carrier of genetic information. The proteins were the obvious choice, as they had a more diverse structure, and thus appeared capable of carrying more information.

This conjecture was disproved as a result of experiments carried out by two bacteriologists working on either side of the Atlantic. Back in the 1920s in London, Fred Griffiths had carried out experiments on pneumocci, the bacteria which causes pneumonia. Under the microscope, the surface of a colony of pneumocci cells appeared shiny and smooth when they were infectious, but when they were non-infectious the surface of the colony appeared rough. If the smooth infectious pneumocci were heated they were killed, becoming rough and non-infectious.

When Griffiths injected mice with either non-infectious rough cells or non-infectious heat-killed smooth cells, the mice naturally remained unaffected. But if he injected the mice with living rough cells *and* heated-killed smooth cells, the mice *were* infected. When he examined these mice, he found that they contained infectious smooth cells. These had evidently reconstituted from a mixture of the two injected cells. Something in the dead cells had caused this transformation in the living ones. A non-living constituent of the smooth cells was evidently capable of combining with an element of the rough cells.

Further investigation showed that this change was permanent. It was inherited by the next generation of cells. Some non-living chemical had transferred and altered the living gene.

The American bacteriologist Oswald Avery, working at the Rockefeller Institute in New York, set about trying to isolate this 'transforming principle', as he called it. By 1944 he had shown that it was a nucleic acid. More specifically, it was deoxyribonucleic acid (known as DNA).

By this stage considerable progress had been made on the analysis of DNA, though without realizing its significance. In fact, just the opposite. This negative view of DNA was largely due to the Russian-born chemist P.A.T. Levene, who also worked at the Rockefeller Institute. Analysis had shown that DNA contained four bases: adenine, guanine, cytosine and thymine. These were arranged in varying order along a linking structure:

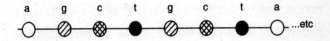

It was thought that genetic information would probably be carried by differing the amounts of each base. But Levene's state of the art analysis indicated that DNA always carried equal amounts of the four bases. He concluded that DNA was a substance of boring structure and little significance. Proteins in the chromosomes were the carriers of genetic information, just as most suspected.

This view should have been exploded by the findings of his colleague Avery, which identified DNA as the 'transforming principle'. But Levene and Avery didn't get on. Temperamentally they were the tortoise and the hare. Levene had a striking, somewhat unsettling appearance: beneath his shock of hair his eyes were masked by tinted glasses. A headstrong workaholic, he was to publish an astonishing 700 papers during his scientific life – and saw himself as the genius–in–residence of the Institute. Avery, on the other hand, was temperamentally retiring: the son of a mystically-inclined, English clergyman. He worked with painstaking exactitude, and didn't believe in making a fuss over his findings. As a consequence, their importance was dismissed by the flamboyant

Levene. To him, Avery's diffidence suggested that he remained unsure of his findings.

However, further analysis by Levene revealed that the nucleic acids had a much more complex structure than had originally been thought. DNA had a 'backbone' consisting of sugar molecules (deoxyribose), linked by a bond (of phosphodiester). Attached to each sugar molecule was one of the four bases.

Such a molecule was very large, and was evidently capable of carrying genetic information. Reluctantly, Avery's findings had to be accepted. The tortoise had its part to play too.

At nearby Columbia University in New York, the Czech chemist Erwin Chargaff immediately embarked upon a further study of DNA. Using quantative analysis, he discovered that different species each appeared to have their own characteristic DNA. Using the latest purification techniques, he managed to isolate the four nitrogenous bases: adenine, thymine, guanine and cytosine. By the early 1950s he had found that contrary to previous thinking, these four bases were not in fact precisely equal. Representing the bases as A, T, C and G, he found that:

$$A + G = C + T$$

also that A=T and G = C

'Chargaff's Rules', as these came to be known, would obviously be essential in future analysis of DNA.

But the fundamental question about DNA still remained. How did this 'transforming principle' actually transform? In other words, how was the genetic information carried, and how was it conveyed? This was the 'secret' contained in DNA: the secret of life itself, and how it passed on from one generation to the next. To understand this, it would be necessary to unlock the structure of DNA. This was the situation when Crick and Watson came on the scene.

CRICK & WATSON

Even at school, Francis Crick had his own attitude towards learning. He showed promise at mathematics, but was mainly interested in the answers rather than the means of reaching them. This attitude was to colour Crick's entire approach to knowledge. With Crick you could always be sure of answers – lots of them, put forward with enthusiasm and conviction, even when they contradicted one another.

Francis Crick was born in Northampton in 1916, the son of a local shoe factory owner. He won a scholarship to Mill Hill, a small public school in the suburbs of London, and afterwards studied at University College, London. Here he was taught the great scientific advances which had taken place at the turn of the century. Unfortunately he was aware that further advances had since taken place, rendering many of these redundant. Crick graduated with a second class degree in physics and an attitude problem. Nowadays these twin attributes would disqualify him from further research – but Crick was not so easily discouraged.

Filled with belief in his own abilities, Crick applied to do research and was quickly allotted a task appropriate to the prevailing view of his character and abilities. His professor 'put me onto the dullest problem imaginable': constructing a spherical copper vessel (for testing water viscosity). Undaunted as ever, Crick remembers: 'I actually enjoyed making the apparatus, boring though it was scientifically, because it was a relief to be doing something after years of merely learning.' Crick had an independent mind, and was intent on doing something with it.

Crick was relieved from filling the world with ball-cocks by the outbreak of war. He was drafted to the Admiralty and set to work designing mines. In 1940 he married.

After the war Crick prepared to return to his research. In 1946 he attended a lecture by the American Linus Pauling, generally recognised as the finest chemist of the century. This awakened Crick to the possibilities of chemical research. Around the same time he also read *What Is Life?* by the Austrian physicist Erwin Schrödinger, one of the founders of quantum mechanics. This book suggested how physics, most notably quantum mechanics, could be applied to genetics. Although many of its brilliant suggestions were later 'modified', even its errors were to prove inspirational amongst the coming generation of post-war scientists.

Organic molecules, the chemistry of genetics, quantum mechanics – this heady cocktail of research possibilities soon replaced the old ball-cocks. 1947 saw Crick divorced and registered for research in Cambridge. Here he set about acquainting himself with the biological side of biological physics. Two years later he was taken on by the Cambridge Medical Research Council Unit at the world famous Cavendish physics laboratory. Thus, at the somewhat mature age of 33, Crick began his first real research work.

Undaunted by the fact that he only had two years biology under his belt, Crick soon became renowned throughout the laboratory for his ability to produce a stream of innovative theories – usually concerning other people's research. Crick had at last found his vocation, and nothing could stop him. It quickly became obvious that an exceptional mind was developing – to say nothing of an exceptionally loud voice and a booming laugh. Some found his company refreshing, in limited quantities; others found his very presence gave them a headache. Amongst the latter was the head of the Cavendish, the ageing Sir Lawrence Bragg, who at 25 had been the youngest Nobel Prizewinner ever. A couple of years later a young American called James Watson arrived at the Cavendish.

James Dewey Watson had been born in 1928 in Chicago. A child prodigy, he had been 'discovered' by a local TV producer who put him on the *Chicago Quiz Kid Show*. At the age of 15 Watson was enrolled at the University of Chicago to study zoology. He wasn't keen on this subject (his real interest was in ornithology), and according to one of his teachers he remained 'completely indifferent to anything that went on in class; he never took any notes and yet at the end of the course he came top of the class'.

At the age of 19 Watson graduated and went on to the University of Indiana at Bloomingdale. Here he was affected by two crucial events. He too read Schrödinger's *What Is Life?*, which had a profound effect. The genius had discovered the gene, and he knew at once that this was his subject. But he was hardly qualified to pursue research in this area. As he admits: 'at the University of Chicago I was principally interested in birds and managed to avoid taking any chemistry or physics courses which looked of even medium difficulty'. With the blithe insouciance of youth (affecting both genius and dunce alike) 'it was my hope that the gene might be solved without my learning any chemistry'.

The second influential event in Watson's life at this point was studying with the microbiologist Salvador Luria, who had fled to America from Mussolini's Italy. Luria was a founder of the Phage Group, consisting of leading geneticists investigating self-replication at viral level. Viruses were thought to be a kind of naked gene, and the simplest viruses are bacteriophages – often known simply as phages. Luria was making important advances in this field, using X-ray irradiation.

Schrödinger had shown Watson the direction, Luria showed him how to go about it. Watson launched into a doctoral thesis on phages, with Luria as his supervisor. Initially Luria was not bothered by Watson's lack of chemistry. Indeed, according to Watson: 'he positively abhorred most chemists, especially the competitive variety out of the jungles of New York City'. So Watson settled down to write a thesis on phages. However, by now Luria was beginning to wonder if the real nature of phages (and thus also of genes) would only become clear when their chemical structure was understood. So he suggested that Watson should at least try and pick up some chemistry.

Watson followed his mentor's advice with enthusiasm, and embarked on a do-it-yourself chemistry course. The results were spectacular, though not in quite the same way as his usual academic results. After Watson attempted to warm up some volatile benzine over a naked flame, he was no longer welcome in the labs. From then on, his chemical knowledge remained largely theoretical.

In 1950 Watson received a fellowship from the

Merck Foundation, to study bacterial metabolism in Copenhagen under the supervision of the biochemist Herman Kalckar. A curious choice, considering his supervisor's profession. But Watson evidently thought otherwise: 'Journeying abroad initially appeared the perfect solution to the complete lack of chemical facts in my head.' Only when he found that Kalckar's English was completely unintelligible did he begin to have doubts about this enterprise. These deepened when Kalckar announced one day that his wife had left him and he was no longer interested in thinking about the digestive systems of bacteria.

Kalckar decided to get over things by spending a couple of months at the Zoological Station in Naples. He asked Watson if he'd like to come with him. This time Watson appears to have had no difficulty understanding his boss's English. He immediately wrote off to the Merck Foundation for $200 travelling expenses.

On an icy spring day in Copenhagen, the emotionally unbalanced biochemist and his non-chemist assistant set off for the sunny Mediterranean. This seaside break at the Merck

Foundation's expense was to prove the most for-
tuitous inspiration of Watson's scientific life.

During Watson's stay in Naples, the city
hosted an international scientific congress with 'a
small number of invited guests who did not
understand Italian and a large number of Italians,
almost none of whom understood rapidly-spo-
ken English, the only language common to the
visitors'. Here Watson met the 33-year-old New
Zealander Maurice Wilkins, who was based at
King's College, London.

Wilkins had been a high-flying physicist, and
during the war had worked in California on the
Manhattan Project, which created the first
atomic bomb. The result had left him disillusioned with physics, and after the war he had
become interested in molecular biology. On
returning to Britain, Wilkins had joined the
Medical Research Council's biophysics unit at
King's College. Here he had begun taking X-ray
diffraction pictures of DNA. He had even
brought one of these with him to Naples, and he
showed this to Watson.

Wilkins' photo depicted a somewhat blurred
geometric pattern, whose significance had to be

pointed out to Watson. In a flash, Watson decided that this was what he had been looking for. This was the way to discover the chemical structure of DNA.

Despite knowing even less about X-ray diffraction than he did about chemistry, Watson wrote to the Merck Foundation demanding a transfer to the Cavendish Laboratory in Cambridge. Here the Medical Research Council had another X-ray diffraction unit, which had been recommended by Wilkins.

Copenhagen, Naples, Cambridge – all within the space of a year. The 22-year-old whizz kid was certainly whizzing around. But what was he whizzing *about*? The Merck Foundation cut Watson's grant by a third, to $2000, and told him this would end six months early in May 1952 (just before the European summer touring season got under way).

The Foundation was determined that this time Watson should stay put. They needn't have worried. With the megalomaniac vision of youth, Watson had now seen precisely what he wanted to do. He would solve the secret of life, no less. He would discover the structure of DNA and become world-famous. This was ambition pure and simple. A few days after his 23rd birthday the quiet, seemingly shy young Watson entered the Cavendish Laboratory in Cambridge.

It wasn't long before he met up with the owner of the famous laugh. The rapport with the 35-year-old Crick was instantaneous. Watson was soon describing Crick as 'no doubt the brightest person I have ever worked with and the nearest approach to Pauling [the great chemist] I have ever seen . . . He never stops talking or thinking'. Crick appeared equally impressed by Watson: 'He was the first person I had met who thought the same way about biology as I did . . . [he had] exactly the same ideas as I had, but I cannot remember in detail what they were'. This is not surprising. At the time, Crick had only been studying biology for two years, whilst the young Watson already had a PhD in the subject.

The gangling unsophisticated young American and the bumptious loud-mouthed Englishman may have appeared different in many ways, but they undeniably had one thing in common: overweening self-confidence. The X-ray diffraction unit at the Cavendish was studying the structure of protein; but Crick and Watson quickly decided that this was not the central issue. What *they* were interested in discovering was the structure of DNA.

Between the two of them, Crick and Watson mustered a considerable range of ignorance for this task. Crick had only two years biology; Watson had no chemistry, and no X-ray diffraction experience. They were unlikely to be hampered by any excess intellectual baggage in their discussions.

These discussions soon began taking place on a regular basis. They would begin in the morning over coffee in their shared office. They would continue over lunch in the Eagle, a popular undergraduate pub, where Crick introduced Watson to the joys of warm flat English beer. And often they would even continue over dinner at Crick's tiny flat, where he lived with his new half-French wife, Odile. These conversations were not confined to Crick and Watson, they frequently involved any of their Cavendish colleagues who would listen.

The Cavendish in Cambridge, along with

King's College in London, were at the cutting edge of X-ray diffraction. The Cavendish had already once changed the face of science. Several decades earlier Rutherford and his colleagues had founded nuclear physics, bringing this new science to fruition with a miraculous burst of creativity at the Cavendish during the 1930s. Now it was the turn of molecular biology. And this was to be largely due to X-ray crystallography.

The head of the Cavendish, Sir Lawrence Bragg, had played a leading role in the founding of X-ray crystallography, along with his father Sir William Bragg. This was the technique which had enabled human vision to extend beyond the range of light. No matter how powerful a microscope is constructed, it can only see objects larger than the wavelength of light. X-rays are a form of electro-magnetic radiation which has a wavelength 5,000 to 10,000 times shorter than the wavelength of light (which itself has a wavelength of $1/10,000$ or 10^{-4} cm). This makes the wavelength of X-rays similar in size to the distance between atoms in crystals.

When a fine beam of X-rays is passed through a crystal, the beam is diffracted by the atoms in the crystal and emerges as a complex pattern. If this pattern is recorded on a photographic plate, it is possible to try and deduce the structure of the crystal. This process may appear relatively simple, but it in fact involves a host of excruciatingly exacting and sophisticated techniques. These involve such tasks as positioning, refining and isolating the individual crystals, as well as attempting the deduction of highly complex molecular structures from dim patterns.

The X-ray crystallography unit at the Cavendish was led by the Viennese-born biologist Max Perutz, who had left Austria in 1936. For several years Perutz's formidable experimental abilities, assisted by Bragg's equally formidable theoretical skills, had been devoted to determining the structure of haemoglobin (the protein of red blood cells). By 1951 they were at last beginning to achieve some success.

But Perutz and his team were not the only ones interested in this topic. The 50-year-old master Linus Pauling was also trying to work out the structure of complex biomolecules. Working from his base at Cal Tech (the California Institute of Technology) he had already deduced a model structure for proteins involving a helix – a spiral of molecules much like a corkscrew. He suggested that this might be the form of many complex biological molecules, including DNA. And in 1951, working from old pre-war X-ray diffraction plates, he even went so far as to publish a suggested structure of DNA, involving three coiled helices.

At the Cavendish Crick and Watson studied Pauling's suggestion, but remained unconvinced. Pauling simply hadn't filled in enough details. His idea was really little more than a brilliant hunch.

Meanwhile things were also progressing at Wilkins' X-ray crystallography unit in King's College, London. Unlike our two free spirits at the Cavendish, this was where the actual work on DNA was meant to be going on. (King's and the Cavendish had a gentleman's agreement: protein was Perutz's baby, DNA was Wilkins'. But Crick and Watson were far too interested in DNA by now to worry about being gentlemen.)

Wilkins had by this stage been joined by the 29-year-old Rosalind Franklin, who had just completed four years X-ray diffraction work in

Paris, and was very much state of the art in this new field. Franklin's arrival should have been a lucky stroke for Wilkins. She was both highly intelligent and attractive, even if she did choose to dispense with make-up and wear somewhat dowdy clothes. But this was 1950s Britain, very much a Stone Age where relations between the sexes were concerned. Quite simply, Wilkins had no idea how to deal with a woman in his laboratory. And 'Rosy' Franklin was no ordinary woman. The wilful daughter of a cultured Jewish banking family, she had her own ideas about how things should be run. Right from the start there was 'chemistry' between the bachelor Wilkins and the unmarried Franklin. Unfortunately, it was negative chemistry. And to make matters worse, Franklin arrived under the impression that she was taking over the X-ray diffraction work on DNA. Wilkins, on the other hand, thought she was being taken on as his assistant. Wilkins and Franklin began working in difficult tandem.

As if all this wasn't enough, DNA was proving a particularly tricky subject for X-ray diffraction. It was a macromolecule, which had to be studied intact, as many of its most significant qualities were lost in any other form. Wilkins had received a particularly pure sample of DNA from Berne. This sample resembled treacle. As Wilkins explained, when a glass rod was raised from its surface 'an almost invisible fibre of DNA was drawn out like a filament of a spider's web'. In this fibre individual molecules were aligned, and although DNA was not strictly crystalline this didn't seem to matter. When much of the water was withdrawn from DNA, its structure exhibited orderly, repetitive, quasi-crystalline qualities, which proved amenable to X-ray crystallography. This water-reduced form was known as 'A-form' DNA, and was the sort initially used at King's.

By November 1951 Franklin had made significant progress. She had worked out a new method of reintroducing water to the A-form DNA. After rehydration the structure of the DNA was transformed. The differences showed up in X-ray diffraction patterns. Franklin had managed to obtain some of the best pictures so far. Even so, these remained very blurred, resembling a film of a spinning four-bladed propeller.

After measuring the angles and patterns that could be deduced from the photographic plates, Franklin began a mathematical analysis of the results. She soon came to some important conclusions about the overall structure of DNA.

Franklin decided to make public her findings at a seminar in King's. Wilkins invited along Watson, knowing from their meeting in Naples that he was interested in DNA. (Though alas, Wilkins seems to have had no inkling of *how* interested Watson was in DNA – he didn't realise that Watson and Crick were planning to 'scoop' him.)

So that he would be able to understand what Franklin was talking about, Watson hurriedly set about learning some crystallography (which is what he was meant to be doing at the Cavendish, in the first place). He then set off for London to attend Franklin's seminar.

Here he learned that Franklin's results seemed to confirm that DNA was helical. In her view, it consisted of anything from two to four interlaced helical chains. Each helix had a phosphate-sugar backbone, with attached bases (adenine, guanine, thymine, cytosine), much as Levene had suggested (see page 34). But importantly, it looked as if the bases were attached to the inside of the helix, possibly forming links between the helical chains.

After the seminar, Wilkins and Watson had a Chinese meal together in Soho. Here Wilkins spilled the beans about the misery of life in the lab with Franklin. This was very much like an archetypical 1950s English marriage. Wilkins apparently withdrew into a shell of distant politeness, while Franklin adopted a cold insistent manner. There was precious little intercourse between them. To Watson, this didn't look like the team that was going to deliver the baby.

Watson returned to Cambridge on the night train in an inspired mood. Franklin didn't seem to be interested in trying to make a model of DNA. All she seemed intent on doing was making painstaking measurements of the diffraction plates, and trying to match them with known bond lengths between molecules. Her method was built on facts.

This just wasn't Watson's way of working at all. Following in the footsteps of his great compatriot Pauling, Watson believed in making models. Admittedly, this could be a bit of a hit and miss procedure. After you'd built up the jigsaw, the diffraction pictures often didn't fit. This meant twiddling a bit with the chemical bonds until they did. Here Watson's bible was Pauling's *The Nature of the Chemical Bond*, the greatest chemistry textbook ever written. This contained a blueprint for the structure of complex biological molecules at bond level.

Crick was another one who didn't believe in wasting time on unnecessary research. After all, theoretical speculation was his forte. (As they knew only too well in the Cavendish: Crick was always poking his nose into other people's experiments, and coming up with instant theories. What was so galling was that his theories were usually brilliant – and sometimes even right.)

Unfortunately, Crick and Watson's model-building soon ran into a few local difficulties. For a start, it depended heavily upon Watson's suspect grasp of X-ray crystallography. In particular, his understanding of what Franklin had said at her seminar. Without further ado, Watson and Crick plumped for building a model with three interlinked helixes. (After all, there was a three to one chance here.) But when it came to the question of whether to attach the bases to the inside or the outside of the helical chains, they definitely backed the wrong horse. They put the bases on the outside – presumably because Watson had forgotten, or misunderstood, what Franklin had said.

The trouble was, Franklin was dealing with the facts – and it was unwise to ignore these, if you wanted to come up with the right answer. Watson evidently didn't look at things quite this way. But Crick did. He was well aware of Franklin's devotion to the facts – but he had his own oblique view of this matter. He suspected that Franklin didn't know what she was doing. In his view, all the evidence necessary for determining the structure of DNA was quite possibly already in existence – lying amongst her diffraction photos.

Crick and Watson made an ideal Laurel and Hardy. Despite an age gap of 12 years, this was a partnership between equals. Both were brilliant at their chosen field (of which the other knew practically nothing). So neither felt behoven to the other. Ignorant, but original suggestions could be made, uncluttered even by the misconceptions gained from half-knowledge. And these could be dismissed by the other, without any hurt feelings. Yet there were moments when such misguided suggestions could prompt a hitherto unconsidered line of expert thought. As a result, when Crick and Watson were good they were *very* good – and when they were bad they were laughable.

But they were aware of this (largely, one suspects, because this was a permanent situation with Crick). This was very fortunate, because the model they originally came up with had precious little to do with reality.

Oblivious to this state of affairs, Crick and Watson proudly invited Wilkins and Franklin to Cambridge for the day. They wanted the King's team to look over their brilliant new model for DNA. This was quickly exposed by Franklin as a joke – though she herself remained unamused at this waste of her time. Growing more irritated by the minute, she fired off one question after another, each appearing to expose a new flaw. The model just didn't fit the X-ray evidence. At all. Then it became clear that Watson had mis-understood something even more fundamental at Franklin's seminar in London. The A-form DNA which Franklin used was dehydrated. In order to build up the true structure of DNA, one had to allow for added water. Watson had done this, all right. But he'd got the figure wrong – woefully wrong. Their model had *a tenth* of the water it should have done.

The subsequent lunch in the Eagle was a sticky affair. Franklin was like a thundercloud; her unwilling partner Wilkins just wished he wasn't there; Crick attempted a little light bombast over his beer; and Watson sat squirming with uncharacteristic embarrassment over his glass of dry sherry.

By the time they returned to the lab, Crick felt more like his old self. In ebullient mood, he refused to surrender without a fight. Watson gamely offered a little, rather lame support, while the others stood in silence. Then Wilkins suggested that he and Franklin might be able to catch the early train back to London, if they hurried. The day was over.

Inevitably news of this debacle soon reached Bragg. The boss of the Cavendish was also not amused. Bragg already had it in for Crick, whose very presence continued to give him a headache. Crick was quickly cast as the villain of the piece, leading the young American research student Watson astray. (If anything, it was of course the other way around.)

Bragg demanded to see Crick in his office, and launched into a firm dressing down. Not only had Crick broken the gentlemen's agreement between the Cavendish and King's, but he had endangered further government funding by the

Medical Research Council, which funded both units. Times were still hard in post-war Britain, and many thought that the Medical Research Council was a waste of money. What was the point of the government funding purely theoretical science projects, such as research into the structure of the protein and the gene, when the country had only just dispensed with food rationing?

Bragg began asking Crick a few pertinent questions. What the devil did he think would happen if word leaked out that King's and the Cavendish were in fact duplicating their work, in an unnecessary competition to see who would 'win'? Why, they'd all be out of a job. And if Bragg had anything to do with it, this situation would remain permanent in Crick's case. With the recommendation he was likely to receive from Bragg, he'd be lucky if he ended up researching the chemical properties of aspirins.

Bragg finished by expressly forbidding Crick from doing any further work on DNA. From now on, this would be King's' preserve. Crick was ordered to return to his work on protein, the work he was being paid for. Watson, for his part, was encouraged to return to his own field, phages. He chose to work on the structure of the tobacco mosaic virus (TMV).

That was the end of it. Just before Christmas 1951, the Crick-Watson race for the DNA title came to a full stop. Or so it appeared. But no one had reckoned with the sheer ambition of Crick and Watson, and the lengths they were willing to go to fulfill this.

In retrospect, it is reckoned that Watson had an 'American' attitude towards ambition. On the other hand, Crick was in rebellion against the stuffiness of middle-class England (the discreet breeding ground of that now extinct species the 'gentleman'). Such attitudes would nowadays be largely welcomed, though at the time they were regarded as unscrupulous. And not without some justification, as we shall see.

Watson's project on TMV was in his own words 'the perfect front to mask my continued interest in DNA'. One of the main components of TMV was nucleic acid. In fact its nucleic acid content was a variant on DNA called RNA, but Watson felt sure that this could 'provide a vital clue to DNA'. Crick's attitude was typically forthright. He may have been banned from *working* on DNA, but no one on earth could ban him from thinking about it.

Crick decided to try a new tack. Instead of the four different types of base being attached to the outside of the backbones of coiled helices (as in the previous model), they must in fact be on the inside. But how would there be room for this? Fortunately all four different types of base consisted of flat molecules. Crick decided (again on no evidence whatsoever) that the bases must fit together like two interleaved decks of cards. In other words, they were stacked on top of one another inside the entwined backbones. And if they somehow attracted one another, this would also help hold together the exceedingly long thin threads of entwined helices (the backbones). Speculation piled on speculation like a house of cards.

As part of his new regime of thinking about (but not working on) DNA, Crick began speculating aloud with a few scientific pals over a few beers in the Eagle. Eventually he became deeply involved in a conversation with John Griffiths, a young mathematics postgraduate. John happened to be a nephew of Fred Griffiths, whose 1920s experiments on rough and smooth pneumocci had inspired Avery to prove DNA was the genetic carrier. This link was not entirely coincidental. John Griffiths had a hunch that certain problems of DNA could best be resolved by mathematics, and had already done a few preliminary calculations using known data about the four bases.

As ever, Crick was soon discussing the fundamental problems. Any structure for DNA had to account for (or at least allow for) replication – the process by which it passed on its genetic information. Crick knew that this must somehow involve the coded sequence of four bases, which now seemed to be stacked on the inside of the entwined helices.

Griffiths passed on to Crick some calculations he had done concerning the four bases – adenine (A), guanine (G), thymine (T) and cytosine (C). Griffiths had worked out which of the bases were attracted to one another. According to him, G attracted C, and A attracted T.

In a flash of supreme inspiration, Crick saw that this could be the key to DNA's replication.

If the helical strands parted, they could then become the templates for the formation of complementary strands *precisely similar to the ones from which they had parted.*

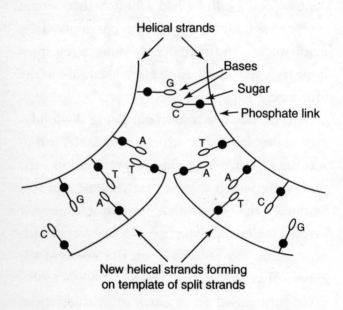

New helical strands forming
on template of split strands

This was indeed a giant leap of the imagination on Crick's behalf – for he didn't understand that Griffiths had envisaged a very different model of his own. Griffiths had based his calculations on the idea that the bases were lined up against each other, edge to edge, and joined by hydrogen bonds.

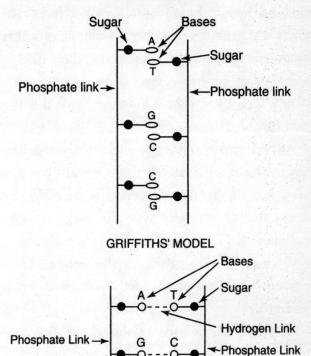

CRICK'S MODEL

Sugar — Bases

A

Sugar

T

Phosphate link → ← Phosphate link

G

C

C

G

GRIFFITHS' MODEL

Bases

A   T   Sugar

Hydrogen Link

Phosphate Link → ← Phosphate Link

G   C

C   G

Another bonus of Griffiths' base attraction combination was that it at once accounted for Chargaff's rules (which decreed that the bases always occurred in the quantities A = T and G = C). Unfortunately Crick remained unaware of this clinching fact – for the astonishing reason that he hadn't heard of Chargaff's rules! (In Crick's defence, it has been pointed out that Watson must surely have referred to these rules at some stage, probably several times – but evidently Crick just wasn't listening. If such is the case for the defence . . .)

All this reveals not only Crick's staggering ignorance of what he was dealing with, but also his equally staggering powers of imagination in being able to deal with it at all under such circumstances. (To say nothing of the sheer bravado involved.) Only a genius at the height of his powers could hope to get away with such effrontery.

There were of course reasons for all this corner-cutting. Both Crick and Watson were well aware that others were on the trail of DNA. They felt certain that they would always be ahead of the opposition at King's (because Wilkins was still misguidedly keeping them informed of their progress). But Linus Pauling was another matter. He had already proposed one rather tentative structure for DNA. It was only a matter of time before he had a real go.

Then Watson learned that Pauling was due to arrive in London for a lecture. Inevitably, Pauling would want to see what was going on at King's. Previously he had only used pre-war X-ray diffraction plates – but once he saw the latest plates there'd be no stopping him.

Crick and Watson could only grit their teeth, and go on pretending to work at their separate projects. The summer term had now started: Watson began playing tennis and taking an interest in girls. In order to differentiate himself from the other crew-cut Americans in Cambridge, he began anglicising his Chicago accent and let his hair grow. Long hair was rare enough in the 1950s, but the results were rarer still in Watson's case. His bushy crop stood on end at great length, giving him an electrically shocking appearance. Only Crick didn't seem to notice, mainly because he was too busy laughing at his own remarks or drinking beer.

But the fates were on Crick and Watson's side. In May the news came through that Pauling wouldn't be coming to England after all. The world's greatest chemist had been prevented from boarding the plane at New York's Idlewild

Airport. At the very last moment the US State Department had withdrawn his passport on the grounds that he might defect to Stalinist Russia. Pauling was an outspoken advocate of a World Peace Conference, and this was tantamount to being a communist spy during the McCarthy era in America.

But it wasn't all good news. At King's, Franklin had made some spectacular advances in X-ray diffraction technique. These had now convinced her that DNA was *not* a helical structure after all. Even Wilkins seemed to concur with her view, albeit reluctantly. (As it later emerged, Franklin hadn't actually let Wilkins see her evidence at this stage. So one assumes it must have been the sheer force of her argument, or perhaps the force with which she put it, which carried the day.)

Watson now completed his work on TMV. According to him, the X-ray diffraction plates showed that this was a helical structure. In fact, his evidence was based on readings which Franklin (who was, after all, the expert) had now decided did *not* indicate a helix.

Despite Franklin's bombshell, Watson went on

insisting that DNA *must* be helical. He was encouraged in this by Crick, who did know what he was talking about. By now Franklin had allowed Wilkins to study her pictures, and he had shown these to Crick and Watson when they visited him in London. One glance, and Crick had decided that Franklin's non-helical theory rested on a misinterpretation. Although the pictures did not show the radial symmetry necessary for helices, in his view this was due to overlapping patterns of crystals. Crick's was a brilliant and daring conjecture – which had the added advantage of agreeing with what he thought was the case. So Crick and Watson remained unconvinced by the world's leading DNA X-ray crystallographer.

Other opinions were not so easily dispensed with, however. In July 1952 Chargaff himself arrived in Cambridge. Crick and Watson badgered John Kendrew, Perutz's brilliant assistant, into arranging a meeting with the great man.

Initially Chargaff was wary. Who were these interlopers, who claimed to know so much about DNA? He was one of the world's leading experts on the subject, and he had never even heard of them. When Chargaff was informed that the young man with the Harpo Marx hair and fake English accent was in fact an American, he understandably decided that he was in the presence of a nut. (In his disarmingly frank account of this period, Watson is not afraid to appear the fool. Yet it is worth bearing in mind, this 24-year-old who was playing the fool was also playing an equal role in one of the major scientific breakthroughs of all time.)

To begin with, Chargaff wasn't quite so certain about Crick. But Crick soon provided him with sufficient evidence to judge his calibre. One can only imagine Chargaff's reaction when Crick unwittingly let slip that he hadn't heard of Chargaff's rules. In order not to waste any further time, Chargaff began asking Crick a few basic questions. In Watson's words 'he led Francis into admitting that he did not remember the chemical differences among the four bases'. Unabashed as ever, Crick explained 'he could always look them up'.

Several years later, Chargaff was to write bitterly: 'Mythological or historical couples – Castor and Pollux . . . Romeo and Juliet – must have appeared quite differently before the deed than after. In any event I seem to have missed the shiver of recognition of a historical moment: a change in the rhythm of the heartbeat of biology. So far as I could make out they wanted, unencumbered by any knowledge of the chemistry involved, to fit DNA into a helix.'

Crick and Watson had done it again. But there was evidently something endearing about this pair of comedians. Even if their enthusiasm may have appeared misguided to many, it was certainly infectious to some.

In the autumn of 1952 Watson made friends with Linus Pauling's son Peter, who had arrived at the Cavendish to do post-graduate research. Peter Pauling was invited to share Watson and Crick's office, and was soon enthusiastically joining in their conversations.

One day Peter Pauling informed Crick and Watson that he had received a letter from his father. Grimly they listened as Peter Pauling told them that his father had once more turned his attention to DNA. He was putting together a paper outlining its structure, and had promised to send Peter an advance copy.

So that was it. Even if they'd wanted to, Crick and Watson knew that they couldn't compete with Linus Pauling. Not under the present circumstances. Any serious attempt on their behalf to arrive at the enormously complex overall structure of DNA relied upon model building, and that was now out of the question. (The terms of Bragg's ban were particularly explicit on this point.) All they could do was speculate on what Pauling might come up with – and this soon proved too galling for words. From then on, the conversations in the office were largely limited to Watson and Peter Pauling – who shared a common enthusiasm for the local Danish au pair girls.

Peter Pauling duly received a copy of his father's paper. After reading it, he passed it on to Crick and Watson. They read that Pauling senior had come up with a structure containing three helically entwined chains with the sugar phosphate backbone *outside* the coil. This was uncannily similar to the one which Crick and Watson had shown to Franklin and Wilkins on their disastrous day trip to Cambridge – except that Pauling had paid a little more attention to working out the details, and matching these to X-ray evidence (to say nothing of making sure that he included the right amount of water).

Despairingly, Watson 'wondered whether we might already have had the credit and glory of a great discovery if Bragg had not held us back'. Even in despair, Watson was still capable of exceptional feats of optimism. But this was only the start. Watson now persuaded himself that perhaps the world's greatest chemist had made a mistake. Suppose he'd botched one of his sums, or made an error in the chemical bonds?

With the obstinacy of youth, Watson settled down to check the precise details of Linus Pauling's structure – the chemical bonds, the figures, the location of key atoms. 'At once I felt that something was not right.' And for once *he* was right. Unbelievably, Pauling had omitted to give the phosphate groups, which formed the links in each chain, any ionization. This meant there was no electric charge to hold together the long thin chains. Without these they would simply unravel and fall apart. Worse still, without this ionization the model which Pauling had proposed for this nucleic acid *wasn't even an acid*.

The world's greatest chemist had made a basic schoolboy howler. (This was even better than Crick and Watson's efforts in this field – the absence of water molecules, the ignorance of Chargaff's rules etc.)

It was obviously only a matter of time before Pauling realised his blunder. Crick and Watson reckoned they had just six weeks to come up with an answer of their own.

The 24-year-old Watson couldn't contain himself over spotting Pauling's gaffe. After telling anyone in Cambridge who would listen, he set off on the train to London, so he could tell them at King's. Wilkins was busy when he arrived, so he burst in on Franklin in her lab (normally a holy of holies where few dared to venture). He at once showed her Pauling's paper, pointing out the error he had noticed. Unfortunately he also felt the need to point out how the great chemist's three helix DNA structure bore an amazing resemblance to the one which 15 months previously he and Crick had proposed (and she had so taken against).

This was an unwise move. Franklin did not take kindly to snide criticism, especially from the likes of Watson (whom she understandably viewed as a conceited young man whose pretensions were rivalled only by his incompetence). Icily containing her anger, Franklin reminded Watson that there wasn't the slightest evidence to support a helical structure for DNA. Watson foolishly began contradicting her, citing evidence from his own work on the tobacco mosaic virus (TMV). This eventually provoked Franklin to such an extent that she emerged from behind her lab bench – apparently bent on attacking him. As she advanced across the lab, the door opened. Wilkins had arrived, just in the nick of time. Watson fled through the door and escaped down the passage. (Discussions about the key to life are evidently just as dangerous in a lab as they are in a pub.)

Afterwards Wilkins comforted the shaken Watson as best he could. He even went so far as to show Watson some of Franklin's latest X-ray work. This was truly amazing. Franklin had managed to obtain X-ray diffraction pictures of an entirely new form of DNA. This B-form, as it became known, occurred when the DNA molecules were surrounded by large amounts of water. This produced X-ray diffraction patterns of astonishing clarity and simplicity.

'The instant I saw the picture my mouth fell open and my pulse began to race,' Watson remembered. It was unbelievable that Franklin was still sticking to her non-helical theory. Admittedly, the A-form DNA evidence was ambiguous; but this new B-form left no doubt whatsoever (in Watson's view). These pictures showed that DNA was unmistakably helical in form. And their amazing clarity pointed to even more exciting conclusions. After a few minutes' calculations, it should even be possible to work out *how many* helical chains there were.

Sitting in the freezing railway carriage on the return journey to Cambridge, Watson excitedly began making sketches and calculations on the edge of his newspaper. By the time he went to bed that night he had decided that DNA con-sisted of two interwoven helical strands.

Next morning Watson was hyper. The moment he burst into the Cavendish no one was safe from his latest ideas about DNA. When Bragg unwisely stepped outside his office, even he received an ear-bashing on the subject.

Instead of going ballistic at this direct contra-
vention of his order, Bragg was surprisingly sympathetic. Quite unexpectedly, he even gave
Watson permission to construct a new DNA
model in the Cavendish. The way he saw it,
there was no longer any gentlemen's agreement
with King's – the main competition was now
Pauling. (Also, Watson had craftily given the
impression that he was working on his own.
Bragg was not yet aware that he had just
sanctioned another bout of Crick at his decibel-
rich best.)

The machine shop downstairs at the
Cavendish was put into immediate production
of metal plates, in shape and scale-size cor-
responding to the four bases. In no time Crick
and Watson set about building up a scale model,
fitting together the intricate structure of two
interlinking helical chains of molecules. If their
hunch about Pauling was correct, they now had
just three weeks left to come up with an
answer.

Everything had to be built up from the basic
building blocks of the known chemical contents
of the complex DNA molecule. The size of each

of the individual molecules which combined to form this complex molecule, and the lengths and angles of chemical bonds between them all had to be taken into account.

An idea of the sheer mind-boggling complexity of this task is given by the following analogy. Imagine a couple of combs, both two metres in length, with uneven teeth sticking out at odd angles. These combs must both be twisted into corkscrews, and then intertwined, so that each tooth on one comb meets up with the complimentary tooth of the other comb. But before even beginning, it is necessary to calculate the exact length, position and angle of each individual tooth of each comb.

An idea of the scale involved is given by the fact that the combined coiled width of the two combs is less than two nanometres. (A nanometre is 10^{-9} metres, in other words one billionth part of a metre.)

As we have seen, Crick and Watson had already put considerable thought into these matters. But other features had to be accommodated too. An important factor was the precise twist of each helical chain of molecules – whether it was coiled closely like a spring, or more openly like a spiral staircase. Watson had surmised from Franklin's X-ray diffraction pictures of B-form DNA that the structure was a double helix, but her data also provided a few even more essential clues. For instance, it was possible to gauge from the patterns on the X-ray plates the exact diameter of the molecule (in the region of 1.6 nanometres). The angle of the ascending 'screws' of the helices and how far they rose in a complete 'circuit' could also be calculated with a much greater degree of certainty.

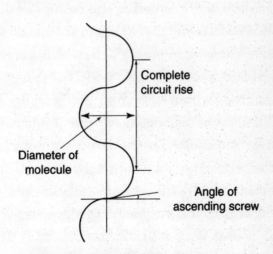

Complete circuit rise

Diameter of molecule

Angle of ascending screw

Gathered from X-ray diffraction picture such as below

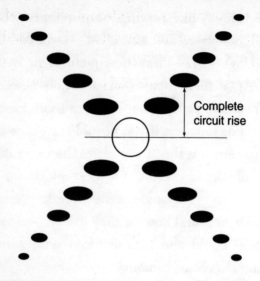

Complete circuit rise

Franklin's new clearer data also meant that Crick and Watson found themselves in an unusual situation. These were precise *facts*, which *had* to be taken into account. If their model didn't fit them, it was they who were wrong, not Franklin. And no amount of fudging could make it otherwise.

Not surprisingly, a few errors were made to begin with. And not surprisingly, given the participants, these were occasionally basic ones.

Against their own previous judgement, Crick and Watson were at first inclined to follow Pauling's suggestion that the bases existed on the *outside* of the entwined helical chains. Luckily, they were both possessed of sufficient self-confidence soon to abandon this conjecture. They had been right; and the greatest chemist in history was once again wrong. The bases had to be on the inside.

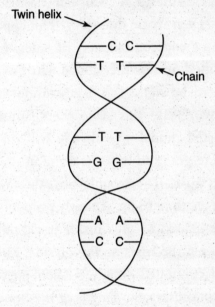

Griffiths had suggested that these bases were attracted to one another C to T, and G to C. But wouldn't it be better, and much simpler, if the bases were attracted like to like? This made for much easier formation of new molecules when the chains split to replicate. It seemed the ideal solution.

Then Watson discovered that the different like-to-like combinations (C+C, G+G etc) were all different sizes. These combinations simply wouldn't fit inside the coiled chains of two regular helices. After a few further calculations he made an even worse discovery. This appeared to be true of *any* combination of bases. None of them fitted inside the coiled chains. Pauling seemed to be right: the 'bases inside' idea just didn't work. By this stage their painstakingly constructed model was already half made, but they were going to have to abandon it and start all over again. The trouble was, they now just didn't have time to build another model.

Crick refused to give up. It just didn't make sense to put the bases on the outside. Hour after hour he continued obsessively fiddling with the model, measuring the length of the bonds again and again, trying to reorganise them so that they fitted inside the chains. As we know, Watson was not one to despair either – but his reaction to the crisis was somewhat different. The tennis season had begun; and also there was a new influx of Scandinavian au pair girls turning up at the parties.

Crick became increasingly irritated as Watson

flitted in and out of the lab, pointing out how Crick's 'inspired' suggestions wouldn't work, before disappearing in search of more congenial bonding arrangements. But Watson was also following his own lines of thought, albeit on a more sporadic basis. In the course of these he made an important discovery. He and Crick could have been making their calculations for the wrong isomeric form of the bases. This was not such a basic error as it might seem. Each base had a molecular formula which allowed for two different molecular structures – the enol form, and the keto form. All the evidence had pointed to the enol form – was it possible this was wrong?

Watson plunged into some lightning calculations, but to no avail. Even in the keto form, when the base pairs joined like-to-like they still didn't fit the chain. Then he discovered that when the keto-form base pairs joined A-T and C-G, just as Griffiths had suggested, they *did* fit inside the chain. And what was more, when they joined in this fashion the two different pairs were identical in shape and size. This meant that either pair could occur anywhere in the chain, thus allowing for a vast permutation of pairs. They'd done it! At last they'd discovered the key to the structure of DNA.

After a series of frantic readjustments, and the odd bit of fine tuning, the model was complete. On March 7th 1953, just five weeks after they had started building, Crick and Watson proudly unveiled their model to their colleagues at the Cavendish. Word quickly began to spread around Cambridge. Within a few days the rumour had filtered out into the academic world at large. Some boffins in Cambridge had discovered the secret of life.

On April 25th 1953 Crick and Watson published a paper in *Nature*, unsensationally titled 'Molecular Structure of Nucleic Acids'. It said all it needed to say in just 900 words and a simple diagram.

Wilkins was characteristically unselfish in defeat, writing jauntily to Crick and Watson: 'I think you are a couple of old rogues . . .' Others were to be less charitable about Crick and Watson's unscrupulous use of material from the King's' X-ray diffraction unit. In their view, Crick and Watson had no right to claim for themselves the credit for this momentous discov-

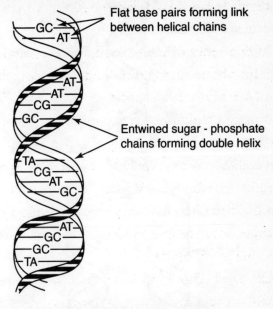

Flat base pairs forming link between helical chains

Entwined sugar - phosphate chains forming double helix

A section of the final DNA molecule arrived at by Crick and Watson : "the structure resembles a spiral staircase with the base pairs forming the steps."

Such views were taken into account by the Nobel Committee. In 1962 the Nobel Prize for Medicine was awarded jointly to Crick, Watson and Wilkins. Sadly, Rosalind Franklin had died of cancer four years previously at the age of 37. To emphasise the joint nature of DNA's discovery, and the assistance given to Crick and Watson by colleagues at the Cavendish, the Nobel Prize

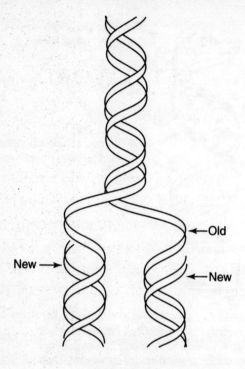

DNA Replication

for Chemistry in the same year was awarded to the head of the Cavendish X-ray diffraction unit Max Perutz and his colleague John Kendrew. Even so, it is Crick and Watson who will forever be linked with the discovery of the structure of DNA.

AFTERWORD

The close relationship between Crick and Watson began to founder somewhat once the public accusations started to fly. Watson soon returned to America, while Crick continued to work at Cambridge. Crick was to remain here on and off for over 20 years, becoming a leading force in the newly opened field of molecular biology. His main work was on DNA replication and how genes carry particular information. He has done much pioneer work on how to crack the 'code' of the DNA bases.

In 1977, at the age of 61, Crick moved to California where he worked at the Salk Institute in San Diego. Crick has also managed to keep up a steady flow of typically 'brilliant' ideas. In 1981 he published a book called *Life Itself*, in which he argued that life on earth originated from outer space. His theory is every bit as off the wall as it seems. (Unmanned rocket arrives from distant part of the galaxy, carrying primitive spores from a super-civilization which evolved billions of years ago. Now read on . . .)

Meanwhile back on planet earth, Crick has also come up with perceptive ideas on the increasingly central question of consciousness (what is it? how does it function? do animals and plants possess it? etc). Crick is still very much alive and laughing.

Watson's post-discovery career has been a similar rollercoaster. Back in America he soon took up a prestigious post at Harvard, where he continued to do research into DNA (particularly its role in synthesising proteins). In 1965 he published *Molecular Biology of the Gene*, which is widely regarded as the best textbook of its kind.

Three years later he published *The Double Helix*, his personal account of the discovery of DNA. Many saw this as an attempt to recapture the limelight. In this he certainly succeeded. His treatment of Rosalind Franklin in this work ensured a public controversy. Yet the book also proved a classic: the finest autobiography of scientific discovery ever written.

In 1988 Watson went to Cold Spring Harbour on Long Island. Here he ran the Human Genome Project, whose aim is to map all the 100,000 human genes (DNA double helices, estimated to contain in all some 3 billion base pairs). Despite proving a brilliant administrator, Watson departed from this project with some acrimony in 1993. Sources differ as to whether he jumped or was pushed. The official version is that he resigned on a matter of principle – because he opposed the idea of patenting genetic information from the project. But according to no less a source than the *Encyclopedia Britannica*, he 'resigned because of alleged conflicts of interests involving his investments in private biotechnology companies'. Either way, when you make one of the major discoveries in the history of science at 25, anything afterwards is bound to seem an anticlimax.

GENETICS: A FEW FACTS, FANTASIES AND FIZZLES

The discovery of the structure of DNA founded an entirely new branch of science – molecular biology. This has resulted in a firework display of new human knowledge. The fuse lit by molecular biology soon exploded into a burst of original technologies and fields of research. Many of these – such as gene cloning, gene banks and DNA identification – were literally inconceivable just a few decades ago. And it's a racing certainty that by the turn of the century the Human Genome Project, or some other branch of DNA research, will produce another of the 20th century's most important discoveries. What this will be, we don't know. Yet it's more than likely that it will revolutionise our entire understanding of what it means to be a human being.

• The Italian nuclear physicist Enrico Fermi once speculated along the following lines:
Our galaxy contains 10^{11} (ie, 100 *billion*) stars, and there are at least 10^{10} galaxies. In the 10^{10} years since the universe began many of these must aeons ago have developed highly intelligent life forms capable of space travel. The earth is particularly favourable to such creatures.

'They should have arrived here by now, *so where are they?*' he asked his Hungarian colleague Leo Szilard.

Szilard replied: 'They are among us, but they call themselves Hungarians.'

• Already we can see *how* to play God, by 'constructing' the DNA structure for any type of individual. One day, perhaps sooner than we think, we might be able to *do* this. But even looking on the bright side, this leads into a paradoxical unknown. We could certainly eliminate disease. We could also aim to produce exceptional individuals – a Picasso say, or the next Einstein, or even another Crick. A genius is by definition the most individual of individuals (deriving from the latin *genius*: that particular quality which is innate to a person or thing). If we can make one, we can clone it. But then individuality ceases to exist . . .

And this is looking on the bright side.

• When asked what the study of biology had told him about God, the geneticist J.B.S.Haldane replied: 'I'm really not sure, except that he must have been inordinately fond of beetles.' There are over 300,000 species of beetles, all of which are truly differentiated species consisting of individual highly complex organisms. By contrast, there are only 10,000 species of birds.

• Concerning the Human Genome Project, Watson wrote in 1990: 'The United States has now set as a national objective the mapping and sequencing of the human genome.' A genome is all the genes contained in a single set of chromosomes, such as a parent donates to its offspring. There are 23 human chromosomes in a human sex cell. Each chromosome contains around 100,000 genes or DNA double-helices. This combined collection of DNA helices contains around 3 billion base pairs.

Watson likened this project to the attempt to put a man on the moon. It is equally ambitious, and will cost a lot less. It is also likely to prove of infinitely more worth to humanity – unless this species is intending to leave despoiled planet Earth for purple pastures elsewhere.

• There are over 4000 inherited human disorders, resulting from genetic defects. These range from sickle cell anaemia to Huntington's disease, and may even play a part in Alzheimer's disease and certain types of schizophrenia. Such diseases can only be treated. At present no inherited disease can be cured.

As parts of the human genome become mapped, we are learning how to change the structure of the gene. This will enable us to prevent such diseases, and much more.

• If homosexuality is the result of an inherited gene pattern, and this can be altered to result in heterosexuality, should this be done? (Imagine vice versa.)

• Entries in scientific encyclopedias now include:

gene amplification, gene bank, gene cloning, gene expression, gene imprinting , gene mutation, gene pool, gene probe, gene sequencing, gene splicing, gene therapy, gene tracking, genetic code, genetic engineering, genetic fingerprinting, genetic mapping . . . These are all happening *now*.

• When the Human Genome Project was set up in the 1980s it was estimated that it would take until the middle of the 21st century to complete. With the advances in computer technology, this was later revised to 2015. Many now believe that this project will be completed before the turn of the century. (The French claim they have done it already, but refuse to let anyone see the evidence in case they pinch it.)

• We know that genetically engineered freaks have already been produced. Genetically enhanced vegetables are already on sale in supermarkets. Farm animals have been 'improved' with a view to better meat production. More disturbingly, a mouse with a human ear growing out of its back has also been bred. And these are just the things we *know* about . . . Frankenstein-type experiments are no longer just fiction. As the molecular biologist John Mandeville recently put it: 'We will be able to produce almost anything except a genetically engineered winning lottery ticket.'

• We only know the function of the 2% of the human genome which contains genes. The purpose of the other 98% remains unknown – the biggest unsolved mystery of molecular biology. One suggestion is that this is a refuse tip for discarded genes, which could even prove amenable to a form of genetic archaeology. (This would allow us to see what we, and indeed life itself, *might* have become.) Another suggestion is that this 'empty zone' is in fact a breeding ground for entirely new forms of genes, and thus provides a kind of ghostly hand on the tiller guiding the direction of life.

DATES IN THE HISTORY OF SCIENCE

pre 500BC	Pythagoras discovers his theorem
322BC	Death of Aristotle
212BC	Archimedes slain at Syracuse
47BC	Burning of Library at Alexandria results in vast loss of classical knowledge
199AD	Death of Galen, founder of experimental physiology
529AD	Closing down of Plato's *Academy* marks start of Dark Ages
1492	Columbus discovers America
1540	Copernicus publishes *The Revolution of the Celestial Spheres*
1628	Harvey discovers circulation of the blood
1633	Galileo forced by Church to recant heliocentric theory of solar system
1687	Newton proposes law of gravitation
1821	Faraday discovers principle of the electric motor

DATES IN THE HISTORY OF SCIENCE

1855	Death of Gauss 'prince of mathematicians'
1859	Darwin publishes *Origin of Species*
1871	Mendeleyev publishes Periodic Table
1884	International agreement establishes Greenwich meridian
1899	Freud publishes *Interpretation of Dreams*
1901	Marconi receives first radio transmission across Atlantic
1903	Curies awarded Nobel Prize for discovery of radioactivity
1905	Einstein publishes Special Theory of Relativity
1922	Bohr awarded Nobel Prize for Quantum Theory
1927	Heisenberg publishes Uncertainty Principle
1931	Gödel destroys mathematics
1937	Turing outlines limits of computer
1945	Atomic bomb dropped on Hiroshima
1953	Crick and Watson discover structure of DNA
1969	Apollo 11 lands on the Moon
1971	Hawking proposes hypothesis of mini black holes
1996	Evidence of life on Mars?

SUGGESTIONS FOR FURTHER READING

James Watson: *The Double Helix* (Penguin) – Best first-hand autobiography of scientific discovery ever written, filled with personal details as well as science. Biased (against Franklin, of course), but a great read for scientist and non-scientist alike.

Francis Crick: *What Mad Pursuit* (Weidenfeld & Nicholson) – A personal view of scientific discovery.

Francis Crick: *Life Itself* (Macdonald) – The off-the-planet thesis.

Robert Olby: *The Path to the Double Helix* (Constable) – A broader, alternative view.

J D Watson and others: *Recombinant DNA, a short course* (Scientific American).